JUNIOR HIGH

#4

JUNIOR HIGH

HOW DUMB CAN YOU GET?

Kate Kenyon

SCHOLASTIC INC.
New York Toronto London Auckland Sydney

ISBN 0-590-40500-4

12 11 10 9 8 7 6 5 4   8 9/8 0 1 2/9

Printed in the U.S.A.   01

First Scholastic printing, May 1987

Chapter 1

"I think I'm in trouble," Nora Ryan whispered to her best friend, Jennifer Mann. "My electric mixer just died."

Jennifer, a willowy girl with raven hair, wiped her grease-smudged hands on a paper towel and sighed. "I'll take a look, Nora, but don't expect any miracles. I can't even get this old toaster to pop up. It just traps the bread and cremates it."

"I don't expect you to be Mr. Goodwrench — just do what you can," Nora hissed. She looked nervously around the crowded shop lab at Cedar Groves Junior High. Mr. Robino, the chubby mechanics instructor with the angelic face, was making his way steadily down the center aisle.

In just a moment, Nora thought desperately, he'll be standing behind us with his clipboard, all set to grade our projects. She could almost feel those dark spaniel's eyes turned sorrowfully on her. One look at the mixer would say it all. "Miss Ryan," he'd mutter, shaking his head sadly, "where have I gone wrong?"

Poor Mr. Robino always took it as a personal failure when a student couldn't master the material in shop. As far as Nora was concerned, the course was a total waste of time. At least learning about nutrition in Miss Morton's cooking class earlier this year had been useful. She was going to be a doctor, not a mechanic!

"You *do* have a serious problem," Jen said softly, and Nora yanked her mind back to the present. "Why did you disassemble the drive shaft from the rotary beaters?"

"Disassemble the —" Nora began, and then stopped. Even though Jen had been her best friend since kindergarten, there were certain times when she drove Nora crazy — like right now, when she sounded as if she had swallowed the shop instruction manual!

"Because those beaters — those things that go round and round — were grinding each other up," Nora whispered tightly. "In another minute, I'd have a counter full of metal shavings!"

"Ah," Jen said, and bent down over the remains of the mixer, her green eyes thoughtful. "So the problem could be directional," she added knowingly. "You know, it might just be something simple like a lock washer or a gasket. . . ."

Nora sighed with relief. "Good, because I've got to get this thing working before — "

"But then again," Jen said cheerfully, "it might be a major malfunction. . . . You know, something that would require a serious overhaul." She tucked a lock of hair behind her ear and grinned at her friend. "We're probably talking two . . . maybe three hours of diagnostic work."

"What!" Nora could feel her voice rising to a dangerous squeak. "I don't have two or three hours. Mr. Robino is going to be here any second!"

A soft cough made both girls spin around. Mr. Robino was standing right behind them, grinning like a Cheshire cat.

"The moment of truth has arrived, my friends," he said in his musical Italian voice. "Mr. Robino is here!"

"I've just had one of the worst mornings of my life," Nora moaned to Lucy Armanson a couple of hours later. She pushed her tray listlessly through the cafeteria lunch line, bypassing the daily specials and heading straight for the salad section.

"Really? What happened?" Lucy's dark eyes were warm with sympathy as she reached for a glass of iced tea.

"I really blew it in shop," Nora confessed sheepishly. "I thought Mr. Robino was going to break down and cry when he looked at the mess I'd made out of my mixer."

"Your mixer?" Lucy arched an eyebrow and shook her curly dark head in surprise.

"My very first assignment was an electric mixer," Nora said sadly. "It had about a zillion parts and a motor that must have been an antique."

"What happened to it?"

"It died in a puff of smoke."

"Are you still talking about your mixer?" Jen asked, suddenly materializing next to the long brass rail that flanked the serving line. She winked at Lucy. "You'd think it was a 747 the way she carried on." Jen leaned over the railing and pointed to the dessert section. "Hey, would somebody grab a piece of that Dutch apple pie for me — I'll pay you back later."

"Dutch apple pie?" Nora piped up. "Do you mean these slabs of overcooked fruit coated with white death?" She picked up a piece of pie and sniffed disapprovingly. "You might as well eat the cardboard plate — it's got the same amount of vitamins in it."

Lucy and Jen exchanged a look. Nora's ideas on health and nutrition were well-known to both of them.

"Just this once," Jen pleaded. "I've got a French test this afternoon, and I need some quick energy." She turned to Lucy. "How about splitting a piece with me?"

"No way," Lucy said quickly. "I'm trying to watch my weight." She tugged at the belt on her crisp, navy wool jumpsuit, and made a face. "Another ten calories and I'll pop my buttons."

Nora stared skeptically at the graceful girl with the model-thin figure. As usual, Lucy looked as if she had just stepped off the pages of a fashion magazine. Her tawny skin was warmed by a touch of coral blush and her enormous eyes were lined with charcoal shadow.

A few minutes later, Nora and Lucy slid into the seats Jen had saved for them at one of the round tables in the middle of the room. It was an unwritten law at Cedar Groves that the center tables — the over-sized ones that could seat twelve kids — were reserved for the eighth-graders.

"So tell me more about this shop class," Lucy said. "I'll be taking it next quarter."

"Then start reading *Popular Mechanics*," Nora said grimly. "Because if you don't know the difference between a carburetor and a crankcase, you'll never make it." She pushed a lock of curly brown hair out of her eyes and spread her napkin on her lap.

"Oh, it can't be that bad," Lucy retorted, tackling her green salad. "You should see what we're doing in home ec — "

"The gingham aprons?" Tracy Douglas asked. "They're a scream! The first time I saw one, I cracked up. I thought I was watching *Leave It to Beaver*, or one of those other fifties' television shows." Tracy's blue eyes were filled with laughter as she looked around the table.

"You're making aprons?" Nora asked. "At least that's something practical."

"Sure, if you're Mrs. Cleaver!" Mia Stevens chortled. "You wouldn't catch me in one of those things — not unless it was a costume party," she added, inspecting one of her long, midnight-blue fingernails.

Mia Stevens and her boyfriend, Andy Warwick, were Cedar Groves's resident punkers, and they made it a point to dress as outrageously as possible. Today, Mia was wearing a black-and-white checkerboard vest over an acid green T-shirt and had wriggled into a pair of yellow leopard-print pants. A gold earring dangled from one ear, and a rainbow assortment of rhinestone studs decorated the other. Her hair was stiffly spiked, with orange tendrils dipping over one heavily mascaraed eye.

Blue-eyed, blonde Tracy stared at Mia across the table and sniffed disapprovingly. All that white makeup, and that vampire lipstick! She looks like something out of *Halloween, Part Three*, Tracy thought, flipping her flaxen hair over one shoulder, and carefully smoothing out a nonexistent wrinkle on her cuff. She knew the frilly white blouse played up her peaches-and-cream complexion, the hand-painted barrettes matched her cornflower-blue eyes, and the trim khaki pants showed off her slim figure. Perfection! she thought happily. Now if only some really cute guy would notice.

"You and Andy looked great at the dance," Jen said to Mia. "It was such a cute idea to come dressed as preppies. Although I think you always look nice . . . just the way you are," she added tactfully.

A loud snort from Susan Hillard made Mia flush. Susan never misses a chance to put someone down, Nora thought angrily. She decided to change the subject — fast.

"Jen, I see you've got a new button," she said swiftly, just as Susan opened her mouth to say something cutting.

"I'm glad someone finally noticed," Jen said, her face lighting up. She tapped a small yellow button pinned to her collar. "Extinct is forever." Her voice was serious.

"Oh, give me a break," Susan said impatiently. "Last week it was the whales. What is this — the Cause of the Month?"

"Extinction involves a lot more than whales," Jen said quietly. "There are plenty of other animals that are in danger, too — mountain gorillas, for example, and elephants, and Bengal tigers."

"Here we go again," Susan said, pretending to yawn. "Lecture number five hundred and thirty-seven."

"Well, some of us are interested," Amy Williams snapped, her brown eyes flashing. "Go ahead, Jen, tell us about the tigers."

Nora watched as Jen's delicate pink-and-white complexion took on a rosy glow. She cares so much, Nora thought. And not just about animals, but about *everyone*. Every month, Jen donated a precious Sunday afternoon to entertain the residents at the Cedar Groves Nursing Home.

And she loved little kids, too. She planned parties and puppet shows at the local orphanage. There's no one like Jen, Nora thought proudly.

When the bell rang, Tracy stood up and said in her wispy little-girl voice, "Well, I know something *else* that's becoming extinct around here, and that's cute guys!" She looked challengingly around the cafeteria, just as a freckle-faced boy with carrot-red hair appeared next to her.

"Oh no," Nora said. "Whenever Jason gets that look on his face — "

"You were looking for cute guys?" Jason Anthony asked, leaning close to Tracy.

"Please, spare me," Susan Hillard cut in. "You're not anybody's idea of a cute guy, Jason. You're not even anybody's idea of a *human*!"

Jason's face contorted with a look of mock pain, and he walked around the table to face her. "You insult a poor messenger — someone who brings you a gift from an admirer?"

"A gift — what kind of a gift?"

"A message," Jason answered mysteriously.

"A message — you mean, you've got a note for me?" Susan asked hopefully.

Jason nodded toward a long table at the back of the cafeteria where Mitch Pauley and Tommy Ryder — two of Cedar Groves's most popular boys — were gathering up their books.

"You've got a message from *them*?" Susan said in a hushed voice. "Well, give it to me!"

"If you insist," he said, grinning evilly

at the rest of the girls. "Put out your hand."

"C'mon, I haven't got all day," Susan said irritably. "On second thought, put it in my pocketbook." She opened her large straw handbag. "Just in case you have some crazy idea of handing me a dead fly or something like that."

"Your wish is my command," Jason said with a little bow. Then, without any warning, he pulled his hand out from behind his back, and plunged it into her pocketbook.

Jen saw a flash of green, and gasped. "What is it? It's not a frog, is it?"

"No, it's not a frog," Susan wailed.

"But what is it?" Jen repeated.

Susan stared inside her pocketbook. "I think it's that slimy stuff that comes in a can. . . . No, it's Jell-O," she said numbly. "He put a whole handful of green Jell-O in my pocketbook."

"I think it's lime," Tracy offered helpfully.

"Well, lime Jell-O is nothing but refined sugar and artificial coloring," Nora added. "It's better to have it in your pocketbook than in your stomach."

Susan looked up slowly and flashed a dangerous sneer in the direction of the retreating Jason Anthony.

Chapter 2

"At least the weather matches my mood," Nora said, squinting up at the flat metallic-gray sky. "Totally rotten."

"Don't tell me, let me guess," Jennifer said, closing her eyes as they trudged down the front steps of the school. "You're still worried about your drive shaft."

"My drive shaft. . . . Oh, is that what you call it?" Nora said wryly. "Let's just say I'm in serious danger of failing small-engine repair. Who'd ever think a mixer would have so many parts?"

"And all of them *moving* parts," Jennifer said sympathetically.

"You mean *none* of them moving — that's the whole problem!" Nora retorted, and Jen giggled. "That mixer was a jinx from the beginning. Maybe I would have done better with some other appliance."

They walked silently for a few moments, each lost in thought. Jen stole a look at Nora, and she could tell that her friend was really troubled. Her brown eyes looked serious, and her mouth dropped dejectedly.

"Look, Nora, it's not the end of the world," Jennifer said brightly. "I'll tell you what — why don't we go back to my house for a couple of hours. Jeff went shopping yesterday, and he bought all the fixings for S'mores."

"S'mores?" Nora said, a trace of the old fire returning to her eyes. "Do you actually think I'd eat a mixture of graham crackers, chocolates, and melted marshmallows?"

"I think a snack would do you good," Jennifer said.

"Okay, you win," Nora said, holding up her hands. "I'll eat S'mores with you and Jeff. But," she added darkly, "I won't enjoy them."

"Delicious," Jeff Crawford pronounced half an hour later. "Here, try one," he said, passing the plate of S'mores to Nora and Jen.

The three of them were sitting around the table in Jen's cheerful blue-and-white kitchen. As usual, everything was sparkling. A lot of people thought it was strange that Jen's dad had hired a male house-keeper after Jen's mother died, but Nora knew that Jeff was the best thing that had ever happened to the Mann family.

Jeff was in his early fifties, and had the kind of sunny disposition that made him fun to be around. He enjoyed kids, and spent hours playing softball with Eric, Jen's younger brother.

"Fantastic," Jen said, reaching for a napkin. "You've got these down to a science."

"You mean an art," Jeff teased her. "Although, come to think of it, I should be an expert by now. I've been making S'mores since I was ten years old. Debby wants me to make a whole batch of them for her Girl Scout troop. She's taking them on an over-nighter in the mountains next weekend," Jeff said proudly.

Nora and Jen exchanged a look. Debby Kincaid had been dating Jeff for the past few months, and Jen always worried that eventually Jeff might marry Debby and move out.

"So," he said, changing the subject abruptly, "are we celebrating or...."

"Commiserating," Nora said wryly. "That was one of our vocabulary words this week, remember?" she said to Jen.

Jen nodded solemnly. "Nora got her very first C today."

"Uh-oh," Jeff said, whistling softly. "That *is* a first for you, Nora." He snapped his fingers. "I bet algebra got you — those quadratic equations will do it every time."

" 'Fraid not," Nora said, reaching for another S'more.

Jeff frowned. "French then? I know you said you were having some trouble with the subjunctive mood."

"No," Nora said, sadly. "It's shop."

"You got a C in shop?" Jeff said incredulously.

"Please," Jen said quickly. "She feels bad enough."

Jeff excused himself to answer the phone, and Nora and Jen looked at each other over their steaming cups of hot chocolate.

Poor Nora, Jen thought, watching her twist a lock of hair around and around her finger the way she always did when she was upset about something. She worries about her grades so much because she knows how tough it is to get into medical school.

Poor Jen, Nora was thinking at the same moment. She'd do anything in the world to help me, but no one can get me out of this one! What if I fail shop? People will think that if I'm not any good at technical things, I won't be a good doctor.

The next day was crisp and cool, and Nora wrapped a bright raspberry scarf around her neck as she was heading out the front door.

"Nice scarf," her sister Sally said appreciatively. "I just may borrow that to wear with my gray jumpsuit this weekend."

"Only if you let me borrow that new sweater from Harrigan's," Nora retorted.

"You've got a deal." A car horn tooted outside and Sally bolted for the door. "Gotta run," she said breathlessly. "We've got an eight o'clock rehearsal." She grabbed a pair of striped leg-warmers off the hall table, along with a pair of battered ballet shoes. "Tell Mom not to wait for me tonight — I'll be late, maybe ten or eleven."

"I'll tell her, but she won't like it," Nora answered.

"Hah! I'll probably get home before she does," Sally retorted. Mrs. Ryan was an attorney for Legal Aid and put in long hours over briefs and papers.

When the front door banged, Nora stood staring at herself in the hall mirror. Physically, she and Sally were completely opposites. Sally was tall and thin, with bone-straight hair that she clipped back in a barrette; Nora was short with a cap of shiny brown curls that swung around her face.

A dancer and a doctor, Nora thought to herself. We're both determined to be what we want to be — and if I only pass shop, I'll make it.

"We're going to do something a little different today," Mr. Robino was saying the next morning in shop class. "Something I think you all will like."

"Maybe he's canceling class," Susan Hillard said in a bored voice.

"Shhh, he'll hear you," Denise Hendrix warned. Denise was a lovely blonde who had caused a sensation when she transferred to Cedar Groves from Switzerland last September. The daughter of a famous American cosmetics tycoon, Denise was a year older and more sophisticated than the rest of her classmates.

Amy Williams turned around to frown at Susan. "What are you griping about?" she hissed. "You got an A on your food processor, didn't you?" She paused and looked at Susan's fingernails — they were impossibly long and painted a frosty shade of copper. "Although how you ever fixed the motor without chipping a nail is beyond me."

Susan's lips curled in a sly smile that reminded Amy of a cat. "Oh, it wasn't that tough," she said lightly. "No one ever checks the model numbers."

"The model numbers?" Amy asked in disbelief. A stern look from Mr. Robino cut off further questions, but her freckled forehead wrinkled in consternation. Had Susan really gone out and *bought* a new food processor, just to get an A? She certainly wouldn't put it beyond her — Susan was capable of anything.

"What did I miss?" Nora said in a low voice, breathlessly taking her place next to Jen. "I got tied up in French."

"Absolutely nothing," Susan sneered from the next counter. "Mr. Robino said he's got some great surprise for us — I'll believe it when I see it," she said, stifling an enormous yawn. "I must have done something terrible in another life to end up in here."

"Don't you like this class?" Jen asked, as Mr. Robino began passing out mimeographed sheets. "I think it's kind of fun," she said cheerfully.

"Fu-u-n?" Susan answered, drawing the word out to three syllables. "Getting our hands filthy from some nasty old appliances? You've got to be kidding," she said contemptuously.

"Well, at least we're learning something practical," Jen said defensively. "When we have our own appliances, we'll know how to fix them."

Susan gave a short bark of laughter. "Sometimes I wonder if you're for real, Jen," she said nastily.

"Omigosh," Nora said, her eyes scanning the sheet that Susan Hillard passed to her. "Jen, he's divided us up into pairs — and we're not together!"

"Who did you get?" Jen asked eagerly.

"Brad Hartley," Nora answered in a stunned voice.

"Brad Hartley — you're working with Brad Hartley?" Susan said increduously. "Leave it to her to get the cutest guy in class," she added.

Nora looked at Jen with an expression of pure panic. Not only was she going to be separated from Jen — she was being teamed up with a *boy*!

A few minutes later, Nora found herself standing next to one of the best-looking boys she'd ever seen. Not only did Brad Hartley have blond hair and clear blue eyes, but he had this fantastic smile that lit up his whole face. When he turned the full force of that smile on her, Nora felt her stomach plummet.

"Hey, that's great," Brad said enthusiastically. "We got a can opener!" He lifted the appliance out of the brown cardboard box and waited for Nora to say something.

"Wonderful," she muttered, trying to put a little feeling in her voice. Wait till this great-looking guy found out how unmechanical she was — she was going to feel like a total idiot. She just knew it!

"I was getting pretty sick of that coffee pot I worked on last week," he said in a husky baritone.

"I guess you had a tough time with it," Nora said sympathetically.

He stared at her, puzzled. "A tough time? Nah, I was just bored with it. It was a snap," he said, flashing a quick grin. "I fix my mom's all the time."

"You do?" Nora gulped.

"Sure. I'll tell you a secret. It's the pump chamber — every time," he said, leaning close. "That's the thing to watch for."

Nora nodded and tried to look interested. "I'll certainly remember that," she promised.

Brad started unscrewing the lever on the can opener, and a half-dozen nuts and bolts fell on the counter. He peered inside at the mechanism and gave a happy sigh. "What a mess. Boy, do we have our work cut out for us!"

Nora tried to fight the sinking feeling that washed over her. "We sure do," she said brightly. She bent over the counter, pretending to match Brad's enthusiasm. This will go down in history as the *second* worst morning of my life! she thought grimly.

Chapter 3

"If I had to choose one kind of food to bring to a desert island, it would be a chocolate-marshmallow sundae from Temptations," Jennifer said with a sigh.

"Not me. I'd pick a cherry vanilla delight," Lucy Armanson insisted, draining the last drops from her frosted mug. "I'd never get tired of these," she added, signaling the waitress for a refill. "Forget dieting. I'd have them morning, noon, and night."

Jennifer, Lucy, Tracy, and Nora were sitting at a back booth in Temptations, the popular ice-cream hangout, enjoying a late Friday afternoon celebration. It was two weeks since Nora had started working with Brad Hartley in shop, and although she was still as much of a klutz as ever, she had to admit that the class wasn't *all* bad. At least she got a chance to spend fifty minutes with one of Cedar Groves's best-looking boys!

Tracy said slyly to Nora, "Your shop partner is a dream! I don't know how you keep your mind on your work with him around. Did you see how great he looked in that blue crew neck sweater today? He reminds me of this lifeguard I met at camp last summer."

As Tracy launched into a long description of her lifeguard, Nora let her mind wander. Brad had been so sweet and understanding to her that morning in shop. As usual, she hadn't been able to make heads or tails out of the diagrams of the can opener, but he had lined up all the pieces for her, and gone through the whole thing step by step. He hadn't even laughed when she asked him where the drive wheel went.

"Right here," he said, putting her hand on the part. "Then when you lower the lever, the cutting wheel engages the can. . . ." He demonstrated for her, and Nora could feel her cheeks flush.

"Oh, now I know what it is," she said, embarrassed. "It's funny how you can use something every day, and never really think about it."

Later, when she and Jen were walking home, Jen looked at her thoughtfully. "You didn't have much to say about Brad Hartley when Tracy was going on about him. Is everything okay?"

Nora nodded. "I just didn't feel like getting into a big discussion with Tracy about him," she explained. A sharp wind whipped around her ankles, and she unconsciously started walking faster. "How are things going with you and Susan?" She knew that Jen was disappointed that the two of them weren't partners in shop.

Jen wrinkled her nose. "You know that line that if you can't say something good about someone, don't say anything at all?" She paused and turned up the collar on her navy blue windbreaker. "Well, let's put it this way — my lips are sealed!"

Another week passed, and Nora came to a surprising conclusion — Brad seemed to *like* it when she was a total klutz in shop! She thought back to the past Tuesday when she knocked over a whole box of screws, which scattered under the lab counter. Mitch Pauley and Tommy Ryder had snickered and called her butterfingers, but Brad just smiled and dropped down to his hands and knees, helping her pick up the screws. And on Thursday, when she accidentally dropped a bolt right into the motor of the can opener, Brad didn't get mad, even though it rattled around for half an hour before they could find it.

"Everyone makes mistakes," he'd said tolerantly, and smiled that thousand kilowatt smile at her. His patience didn't even run out on Friday, when she dropped a hammer on the white plastic casing of the can opener, splitting it wide open.

"At least you didn't drop it on my foot," Brad teased her. "Anyway, it's nothing a touch of glue can't fix," he said reassuringly. He repaired the crack, humming softly to himself, explaining some of the finer points of motor repair to her.

But today something was wrong. It had started out when Mr. Robino mentioned that the choke on his car wasn't working properly. "Does anybody know what a choke is?" he said, his round face beaming.

"Sure. It's a butterfly valve," Nora said automatically.

"Very good, Nora," he answered. "And what's the difference between a manual choke and an automatic one? Why don't we let your partner tackle this one."

Brad, caught off-guard, looked up in consternation. "The . . . uh . . . difference between the two? That's . . . well . . . it's kind of . . . hard to say. . . ." A deep red flush crept up his neck, and he looked like he wanted to disappear into the floor. "I know what it is, but I can't seem to explain it. . . ."

Someone in the back snickered, and Tommy Ryder yelled, "Hey, Brad, take your time, it's a fifty-minute class!"

"It's really quite simple," Mr. Robino said, drawing a diagram on the board. "I'm not an artist, but this gives you an idea. . . . These are the two possibilities." He turned with the chalk still in his hand and nodded at Nora. "And which do you think is better?" he asked, indicating the blackboard.

"I don't like the automatic choke," she said quickly.

"And why is that?"

"Because. . . ." She glanced at Brad, and nearly forgot what she was going to say. He was glaring at her, his features stony. "Because . . . it makes you waste gas," she said finally. "And the wasted gas makes the engine wear out pretty fast." She took another peek at Brad out of the corner of her eye and cringed — if looks could kill, she'd be in her coffin.

"Excellent! I am truly impressed."

Mr. Robino smiled encouragingly at her, and without meaning to, Nora blurted out, "You see, it washes the oil off the cylinder walls — "

"Hey — she thinks she's heading for the

Indy 500!" Mitch Pauley hooted from the last row.

"That's enough," Mr. Robino said sharply. He stared coldly at Mitch and Tommy, while Nora felt herself blushing up to her hair roots. Every time she opened her mouth she put her foot in it! She was grateful when Mr. Robino ordered everyone to open their books just then, and she made up her mind not to look at Brad for the rest of the hour. She just knew that he thought she was some show-off creep!

But as luck would have it, Nora's ordeal wasn't over. Because for the next twenty minutes, Mr. Robino decided to hold an "oral pop quiz" and he called on Nora over and over. She was right in the middle of telling the class that the carburetor was bolted to the intake manifold, when the bell mercifully rang.

"How'd you know all that stuff about fuel pumps?" Brad asked suspiciously, as they were collecting their books and heading for the hall a few minutes later. "We haven't even covered that yet."

"Greg Morton," Nora said quickly. "He taught me everything there is to know about fuel pumps." She paused. "More than I *wanted* to know, actually."

She smiled warmly at Brad, but he didn't

look amused. In fact, if she didn't know better, she would have thought he was still annoyed. But that was crazy, wasn't it? Couldn't he see she was trying to smooth things over?

"And who's Greg Morton?" Brad asked stiffly, tossing his jacket over his shoulder.

"He's . . . he's Sally's boyfriend. Sally's my sister," she said haltingly. "You see, he has this really old VW. . . . He says it's so old, it should be in the Smithsonian." She waited for Brad to smile, and when he didn't, she went on uncomfortably, "Anyway, he spends all his time fixing it up. When he's not fixing it, he's talking about it."

"Yeah?" Brad grunted, pretending to be fumbling with his notebook.

Nora flinched. The temperature in Brad's voice had dropped about thirty degrees. "Anyway," she continued, wishing she had never started this conversation, "I was with Sally and Greg one day when his VW broke down. We were way out on a country road, miles away from a service station, and Greg pulled out this book called *How To Keep Your Volkswagen Alive*. He asked me to read him the chapter on fuel pumps while he fiddled around under the hood."

"You must have a photographic memory," Brad said, turning to face her at last. "Mr. Robino was really impressed." His eyes were cold, and it was obvious he didn't mean it as a compliment.

"I don't think I have a photographic memory," Nora said, wondering why she felt so nervous and defensive. "I guess that chapter just stuck in my mind. You see, it was so important that we get the car fixed and get out of there. Sally had a dance performance coming up that night, and she was really getting nervous. So every word I read about fuel pumps seemed important to me and — "

The second bell rang just then, cutting off the rest of the sentence. Brad scooped his books off the counter, tossed a brief "See ya" over his shoulder, and dashed for the door.

"Wow," Nora said softly as Jen came up behind her. "I think I just put my foot in my mouth. Again."

Later that night, she tried to explain to her mother what had happened with Brad. It was nearly eleven, and the den was quiet except for the ticking of the old mahogany clock on the mantelpiece.

"You're still up?" her mother had said when Nora padded into the den in her red Dr. Denton's. "You should have been asleep an hour ago. You're going to be walking around in a fog all day tomorrow."

Nora smiled. "Hah! What about you? You've been hunched over those books for hours. I don't think you've moved a muscle since we finished dinner."

"You're probably right," her mother said wearily. She pushed aside the heavy legal book and rubbed her eyes.

"Want some hot tea?" Nora offered. "And some of those carob-granola bars I made?"

"Now there's an offer I can't refuse," Mrs. Ryan said gratefully. "Especially if you're going to get it."

A few minutes later, Nora set down two steaming mugs on the den table. She took one and curled up on the sofa next to her mother, wondering how to bring up the scene in shop.

"Mom," she said finally. "Do you think boys don't like girls who are smart?"

"Is this a trick question?" Her mother smiled.

Nora laughed. "I know it sounds crazy, but there's this really terrific boy in my shop class. His name is Brad and he's my partner. Now here's the strange part. At first, Brad was really friendly and helpful to me. He liked explaining things, and he didn't care how many dumb questions I asked him. But now he's suddenly gotten ... well, cool."

Her mother looked interested. "You mean he's changed?"

"Definitely. But I think he's changed because I've changed. Up until now, I've been a total idiot in shop, but today we happened to hit on something I knew a lot about. ..."

"You knew more than Brad," her mother said wryly.

"That's right. And — "

"And he couldn't take it," her mother finished for her.

Nora stared in amazement. "Sally always said you were a mind reader."

"I'm afraid not," Mrs. Ryan said smilingly. "Just an educated guess."

"A guess?"

"Sure." She reached out for her mug of tea and tucked her long legs under her. "The same thing happened to me when I started law school."

"It did?"

Mrs. Ryan laughed and tucked a cushion behind her back. "I was hopeless at tax law, and I was working on a brief with a guy who was a genius. As long as he knew more than I did, everything was fine. He had all the patience in the world — "

"Just like Brad," Nora said under

her breath. "What happened?"

"What happened," Mrs. Ryan said, "is that I began studying tax law like a maniac. By the next semester, I knew more than Bernie did. And you know what — he couldn't take it! His whole attitude changed."

"That's rotten!" Nora protested.

"It sure is," Mrs. Ryan said agreeably. "But the question is, What are you going to do about it?"

Nora bit her lip thoughtfully. "I don't know," she said truthfully.

The very next day, Nora found herself back in the limelight in Mr. Robino's class. It started out harmlessly enough, when Mr. Robino started reminiscing about a physics class he had once taught.

"Now there was a challenge!" he said, his face crinkling in a giant smile. "Just try explaining the first law of thermodynamics to thirty-five college freshmen!"

"Heat is work, and work is heat," Nora said softly to herself. To her amazement, Mr. Robino stopped dead in his tracks and stared at her.

"You are an amazing young woman, Nora," he said seriously. "That is exactly the right answer."

Nora flushed. She hadn't even realized

she had spoken the words aloud! Now what was she going to do?

Before she had a chance to think about it, Mr. Robino had raced to the board and written the phrase in giant letters. "A very important concept," he said thoughtfully. "Where did you learn it, Nora?"

"I . . . uh, don't know," she mumbled, embarrassed. "I must have read it somewhere."

"Sure," Brad muttered under his breath. "Probably in a Volkswagen book."

Nora didn't dare look at him, and pretended to be flipping through her shop manual. Why didn't Mr. Robino just drop it and get on with the class? The last thing she wanted was to be singled out for any more special attention. She wanted to be invisible.

But Mr. Robino was still staring at the blackboard transfixed. "This law applies to virtually every engine you can imagine," he said quietly. "If only we had time to pursue it. . . ." Someone cleared their throat, and he stepped back reluctantly. "That's the trouble, there's no time for theory," he said sadly. "Okay, everyone, turn to page thirty-six."

Nora gave a sigh of relief. She was off the hook for the moment, but she knew that the damage had already been done.

Chapter 4

"You don't think I'm imagining it, do you?" Nora asked Jen and Tracy the next day after school. They had just finished window-shopping in Twin Rivers Mall and were sharing a half-pepperoni, half-green-pepper pizza at Luigi's.

"No, I don't," Tracy said firmly. "If you think Brad's angry, he probably is."

"The evidence is pretty overwhelming," Jen said sympathetically.

Nora had to agree. Today in shop, she'd come up with a good definition of centrifugal force, and for a moment had felt a wild rush of satisfaction. Then she glanced at Brad's face and had stopped smiling abruptly. He looked tense and upset, as if she'd betrayed him.

"But the whole thing just doesn't make sense!" Jen blurted out.

"Oh, yes, it does," Tracy insisted. She

paused to look at two boys wearing varsity sweaters who were standing at the takeout counter. They were practically clones with identical short haircuts, broad shoulders, and dazzling smiles.

"The Holloway twins," Nora said automatically. "They're too old for you."

"Gosh, what are you getting so uptight about? I was just *looking*," Tracy protested. "I think they had their picture in the paper last Sunday."

"Tracy," Jen reminded her gently, "we were talking about Nora."

"I was getting to that," Tracy said, running a hand through her silky blonde hair. She leaned forward to take a final look at the twins before turning her attention back to her friends. "The thing is, Nora," she said, sinking her white teeth into a piece of pepperoni pizza, "boys *never* like girls who are smarter than they are."

Nora and Jen exchanged a look and burst out laughing. "I can't believe you really said that!" Nora exclaimed. She reached for a napkin. "My mother said that happened to her once, but that was a long time ago. No one really thinks like that *now*!"

"That's right," Jen agreed. "It's ancient history. Ms. McNamara found one of those old *Tips for Teens* books and brought it into sociology class. It was a riot. She read us a section that said girls should let boys win at tennis, so their male egos don't get bruised."

"What's so terrible about that? I would always let boys win at tennis," Tracy said. Nora and Jen groaned and Tracy held up her hand. "Okay, you can make fun of me all you want, but deep down, you know I'm right." She whipped out her compact and touched up her pale peach lip gloss. "If you want to get something going with Brad Hartley, Nora, you better take my advice."

"And that is —"

"Play dumb." Tracy smiled and slipped her leather shoulder bag over her arm. "Believe me, it works every time!"

"It's always a challenge talking to Tracy," Nora said later as she and Jen made a quick stop at Jeans City. "Sometimes I think she's living in the wrong century."

"I know what you mean," Jen agreed.

Nora stopped to look over a pile of yellow-and-black animal-print pants that were on sale. "These are really going to be big this spring. *Seventeen* just did a feature on them."

"So get some," Jen urged. She bypassed a pile of pastel shaker knit sweaters and headed for the rack of oversized blouses. "Mia Stevens wears them all the time."

"She can get away with it, but I can't," Nora said regretfully, shaking her head. "You've got to be tall and skinny to wear this stuff."

"I don't know about that." Jen shrugged. "I may get a pair myself."

"Well, sure. On you, they'd look great," Nora told her, "but I'd look like a giant bumblebee."

"No you wouldn't," Jen said, holding up a canary-yellow blouse. She looked at the price tag and frowned. "What do you think? It's three weeks' baby-sitting money."

"Easy come, easy go," Nora told her, snapping her fingers.

"Hah! Have you ever sat for the Martin twins?"

Nora thought Tracy's suggestion to "play dumb" was ridiculous, of course, but there was still a nagging doubt in her mind about the way she had handled the whole thing. She hadn't been showing off in shop — she really *did* know a lot now. But why had Brad seemed so threatened? Her mother would say that it didn't matter how Brad felt — if he was insecure, that was his problem. But, Nora glumly admitted, she *liked* Brad Hartley, and she was *beginning* to like shop. So now it was her problem, too.

"I want to pick up a copy of *Teen Beat*," Jen said, breaking into Nora's thoughts. "Is it okay if we stop at the Briarpatch on the way home?"

"Sure," Nora agreed. The Briarpatch was Cedar Groves's oldest bookstore, and she and Jen loved to wander through the crowded aisles, looking over the new paperbacks.

Today they ran into Steve Crowley, poring over a cookbook display near the front of the store. Tall and good-looking, with dark brown hair, Steve had been friends with both girls since kindergarten. Tracy often asked Jen and Nora why they had never dated him — after all, he was a hunk — but as Jen said, "you just don't get romantically involved with someone you shared your *fingerpaints* with!"

Nora stopped to talk to him, but her attention wavered when a large wall display caught her eye. "Steve, look," she said excitedly, "they have books on mechanics!"

"Sure, but what's the big deal?" He gave a bemused smile as she dragged him over to a section on automotive repair.

She looked at Steve, her brown eyes bright with excitement. "And here's one that tells you how to build your own patio."

"You really want to build your own patio?" Steve asked with amazement. "Nora, if I remember, you don't even like to change a light bulb."

"Well, that's all in the past," she said breezily. "I've suddenly gotten interested in mechanics and fixing appliances and things like that."

"Oh yeah — since when?" Steve challenged her.

"Since I started taking Mr. Robino's shop class," she said.

"Oh, now I get it." Steve laughed. "I've heard it's not as much of a snap course as people think."

"It's not a snap course at all," Nora said. "You know, I've actually found myself getting interested in some of this stuff. It's kind of fascinating, once you start reading it."

"If you say so," Steve said dubiously. He glanced at his watch and zipped up his jacket. "I've got to go, but do me a favor, Nora. . . ."

"Yes," she said, already scanning the rows of titles.

"Please don't build one of these," he said, holding up a book with a sun deck on the cover. "Somehow, it's just not . . . you!"

Later that night, Nora was propped up

in bed with a home-improvement book when the phone rang.

"Hi, Jen," she said, without waiting for the caller to identify herself. She and Jen called each other every single night between eight-thirty and nine o'clock. It was a ritual they had started when they were in third grade. No matter how much time they had spent together during the day, neither one could go to sleep without having one more chat.

"I bet you're right in the middle of French verb conjugations," Jen said brightly.

"Wrong, Jean Dixon," Nora laughed. "I'm right in the middle of an electrical wiring diagram."

"You're kidding!"

"No, I'm not," Nora said. She wriggled her toes inside her long flannel pajamas. "In fact, I've been so involved in this book, I haven't moved a muscle for almost two hours, and . . . ouch . . . my foot fell asleep!"

"It must be quite a book," Jen said.

"Oh, it is," Nora replied cheerily. "Do you know that there are twenty-nine basic mistakes you can make in wiring?"

"Actually, I didn't, but why do I get the feeling that you're going to tell me about every single one of them?"

"It's fascinating," Nora said seriously. Her eyes ran down the page. "Suppose you've got a rest-type circuit breaker...."

I can't believe how excited she is over this mechanical stuff, Jen thought sleepily. Does she really think that Mr. Robino's class is so exciting? No, it must be something else. It must be Brad Hartley.

Jen tucked the phone under her chin, and began to brush her long dark hair. "A hundred, ninety-nine, ninety-eight," she said under her breath. She brushed her hair a hundred strokes every night, and somehow, counting backwards made it seem to go faster. Nora would laugh, and say that was the most unscientific thing she'd ever heard, but Jen didn't care. It was true.

"So the main thing to remember," Nora's voice droned on, "is to make sure the grounded wire is connected to the terminal of the receptacle."

"And the hipbone is connected to the thigh bone," Jen said with a giggle.

"What's that?" Nora sounded annoyed at the interruption.

"I was just thinking out loud," Jen said apologetically.

Nora went on with her explanation, and sorry, Nora." She fumbled in her notebook restful, reminding her of something. What was it? Oh yes, those breakers at the beach last summer. Running lightly into the shore in a burst of white foam, and then flowing out to sea.

Jen's head slipped further down on the pillow, and she didn't even notice when the brush fell out of her hand. A minute later, the receiver on her pink Princess phone rolled over the edge of the bed. She wondered idly why she couldn't hear the voice at the other end anymore, but it was too much of an effort to think about it.

"I can't believe you hung up on me!" Nora said the next morning. Her cheeks were pink from the cold, and she hopped up and down from one foot to the other as they stood on the stone steps outside Cedar Groves Junior High, waiting for the bell to ring. They could have gone inside, but that would be incredibly uncool, as Tracy would say.

"I didn't hang up," Jen protested. "We were talking about circuit breakers, and — "

"Hah! You mean I was talking about circuit breakers — you were snoring!"

"Not true." Jen laughed. "Honestly, I'm sorry, Nora. She fumbled in her notebook and drew out a magazine. "Anyway, I have a peace offering for you." She handed Nora a rumpled copy of *Teen Beat*.

"What is it?" Nora asked suspiciously. She shivered inside her thin red windbreaker and tried not to look as cold as she felt.

"The magazine I bought at the Briarpatch yesterday," Jen said impatiently. "Now, don't have a heart attack, but they have a feature on your very favorite rock group."

"They have a story on Trilogy?" Nora said breathlessly, grabbing the magazine. She flipped quickly through the pages, and stopped at a set of glossy photos. "Fantastic!" she gasped.

"You're welcome," Jen said.

"Oh yeah, thanks," Nora replied, her eyes glued to the page. "Michael Stevens has let his hair grow, and look, Terry Reggles is growing a . . . mustache!"

"Ooh, he's gorgeous," Tracy said, coming up behind Nora and peering over her shoulder. "That's the latest look," she said knowingly.

"And Peter Marks has added another earring," Jen pointed out.

"Do you think so?" Nora squinted and took another look. "No, I think he's always had six."

"Six on the right ear, four on the left," Tracy said dreamily.

"Tracy memorizes this stuff!" Lucy Armanson laughed.

"Is this new?" Tracy asked suddenly, indicating the silver buckle on Lucy's lightweight jacket.

Lucy nodded. She was trying to keep her teeth from chattering.

"It's great," Tracy continued. "Blue's a good color for you."

"Thanks," Lucy said. She ran her hand through her curly Afro. "I was afraid it might be too bulky.

"Are you kidding?" Jen spoke up. "That's the look that's in, isn't that right, Nora?"

"What?" Nora said dazedly. She'd been lost in an exclusive interview with Peter Marks, in which he explained, once and for all, that he liked girls with a sense of humor.

"Lucy's new jacket," Jen prompted. "She's afraid it's too bulky."

Nora forced her eyes off the page long enough to glance at the jacket. As far as she could tell, it looked exactly like Lucy's old jacket, except it was a little lighter. "No, it's just right," she said quickly.

"You can borrow it sometime," Lucy offered.

"What?" Nora said vaguely. She skimmed the page, trying to pick up the thread of the interview. Beauty wasn't important to Peter Marks, he confessed. He preferred girls who had good personalities and were fun to be with. "I like girls who can make me laugh," he said. Then why does he always date famous models? Nora wondered.

"I said, You can *borrow* it sometime," Lucy said, cutting into her thoughts. "The *jacket*," she added, when Nora gave her a blank look.

"Oh, I could never wear anything like that," Nora said innocently. "It's much too bulky." She ducked her head back to the article, and hardly noticed when her friends burst out laughing a moment later.

What's so funny? she wondered, but she didn't bother to pursue it because it was much more interesting to read that Peter Marks made his own granola, fresh every single morning. . . . Amazing, she thought rapturously. We have so much in common!

Chapter 5

"Have you heard about the school trip?"
Jason Anthony asked Nora a few minutes
later as she brushed past him in the hall.
His freckled face was beaming as he
balanced precariously on his skateboard,
zigzagging past the dull green lockers.
Skateboards were strictly forbidden inside
the school building, but Jason assumed,
correctly, that no one would bother report-
ing him.

"What school trip?" Nora said, still
reading the Trilogy interview in *Teen
Beat*. Peter Marks had just confessed that
he had a lifelong passion for health foods,
and was particularly fond of tempeh. Nora
had only a vague idea what that was, and
made a mental note to look it up in the
library.

"There isn't any school trip," Susan

Hillard said gratingly. "It's just this poor boy's idea of a joke."

"No, I'm telling the truth," Jason said, making a dangerous U-turn on the board, and nearly running over Susan's toes. "Scout's honor." When Nora looked at him suspiciously, he grinned. "We can sit together on the bus, if you like. It's a long trip to Washington."

"Washington!" Tracy said, suddenly appearing behind them. "That's miles away. I have a friend who moved out there." She paused, frowning. "Or maybe it was Oregon."

"Not *that* Washington," Jason said. "Washington, D.C. You know, the nation's capital." He hopped off his skateboard and fell into step beside them. "It's going to be very educational," he said slyly. "Ms. Anderson said so."

"Ms. Anderson — what does she have to do with it?" Susan said, interested in spite of herself.

Jason leaned close and lowered his voice. "She's leading the group," he whispered hoarsely. "Along with Mr. Robards."

"Now I know he's making it up." Susan rolled her eyes. "We're waiting for the punch line, creep."

"This *isn't* a joke," Jason insisted. "Nora, you believe me, don't you?"

"I suppose so," Nora said in a weary voice. She wished everyone would stop talking to her so she could get back to the magazine! In just a minute the bell would ring, and then she'd be stuck in history class for the next fifty minutes.

Encouraged, Jason edged closer. "And can we sit together on the bus?"

"Probably," Nora muttered. Someone jostled her elbow and she nearly dropped the copy of *Teen Beat*.

"I can't believe you're falling for this!" Susan snorted. "What's wrong with you, Nora? You're just encouraging him!"

Nora finally looked up, bewildered. "What's she so mad about?" she asked Tracy as Susan turned on her heel and stomped down the hall.

"I'll see you at lunch, Nora," Jason yelled, jumping back on his skateboard. He winked at her as he whizzed by. "We can plan our trip together. Just the two of us."

Trip together? The two of us? Nora was baffled. What in the world was he talking about?

"It's true," Tracy whispered a few minutes later, shaking her head in disbelief. Mr. Robards was busily passing out a pile of mimeographed sheets describing a school trip to Washington, D.C. "And I thought Jason Anthony was just making it up."

Nora half turned in her seat to face her. "Is this what he was babbling about?"

"It sure was," Tracy said in a low voice. She kept her eyes fixed firmly toward the front, and held her lips still, like a ventriloquist. She knew what would happen if Mr. Robards caught her talking in class: She'd be zapped with a three-page report on a current news event. When Mr. Robards glanced in her direction a moment later, she quickly covered her mouth in a fake yawn. He stared at her suspiciously for a minute, and then turned his attention back to the mimeographed sheets.

"You'll have to bring these home to your parents for their signatures," Mr. Robards explained. "The deposit is due on Thursday, and the balance is due two weeks from today. We've tried to keep the expenses down, so as many of you can go as possible." He scanned the room. "Who's been to the nation's capital? Let's see a show of hands."

About half the kids raised their hands, and Tracy said hesitantly, "I've been there, but I was only six months old. Does that count?"

"I don't think so," Mr. Robards said with a laugh. "You probably didn't get much out of it. Haven't you been there, Denise? I know you've traveled all over the world."

Beautiful, blonde Denise Hendrix, recently transferred from Mr. Carpenter's history class, sat with her hands folded on her desk. She always looks like she's just had a manicure, Nora thought. Her perfect nails were painted a frosty beige.

"Actually, no," she said apologetically. "I think I've flown over it, though. I've taken the Concorde between New York and Paris a few times."

"The Concorde!" Mitch Pauley whistled appreciatively. "That thing flies at twice the speed of sound!"

"It must be nice," Tommy Ryder hooted. "Hey, Denise, can I carry your luggage the next time?"

Someone giggled in the back row, and Mr. Robards cleared his throat. "Okay, gang, let's get back to business. . . ."

Denise looked a little embarrassed and didn't notice the admiring look that Lucy Armanson was giving her. I bet she buys her clothes at fancy Paris boutiques — just like the ones we've read about, Lucy was thinking to herself. They'd just finished a chapter on shopping in French class, and Mr. Armand had covered everything from the giant department stores like Galeries

Lafayette, to the famous design studios such as Dior and Givenchy.

Denise was wearing a long cranberry sweater over a pair of black stirrup pants, with tan leather cowboy boots. The sweater was oversized, but Denise had cinched it tightly at the waist with a designer belt made of wooden beads and rough burlap woven together in a thick braid.

Lucy took another look and sighed. With her willowy figure and shimmering blonde hair, Denise managed to look totally different from everyone else. And totally terrific.

"How long will we be gone?" Tracy asked.

"It's all on the paper," Mr. Robards said patiently. "We leave on Friday the twenty-seventh at seven sharp — that's seven A.M.," he added quickly as Tracy started to raise her hand. "That way we'll be sure to get to the capital before dark. We'll check into the hotel, have dinner, and go to bed early so we can get a fresh start the next morning on the museums."

"The Air and Space Museum, the Museum of Natural History, the Washington Monument, the Jefferson Memorial, the Capitol building . . . you've got a dozen places listed here, Mr. Robards. Are we really going to hit them all in one day?" Tommy Ryder asked.

"No, stupid," Mitch Pauley interrupted him. "We've got four whole days in Washington, right, Mr. Robards?" He looked around the room, pleased with himself.

"That's right," Mr. Robards agreed. "We'll have plenty of time to see the major sights, if we organize ourselves. And I forgot to tell you — Ms. Anderson, who, as you know, also teaches social studies, will be joining us on the trip. I think she has a few special places she wants to visit, like Mount Vernon and the Mint, so we may divide you into groups. It won't hurt my feelings if some of you decide to go sightseeing with her instead of with me," he added with a chuckle.

"Mount Vernon — that's where I'm headed," Mitch Pauley said in a stage whisper.

"You really want to see Mount Vernon?" Tommy Ryder asked. "It's no big deal. It's just some big old house filled with antiques — I think George Washington lived there."

"Who cares about Mount Vernon?" Mitch retorted. "Have you seen Ms. Anderson?"

Later, in shop class, Nora came to a happy conclusion: She had a natural talent for electrical wiring! She had just found a faulty connection on an electric fan, and had dangled the split wire in front of Brad triumphantly.

"This was the culprit!" she said, thrilled. "To think that we spent all that time taking apart the motor for nothing. I'm beginning to think that wiring is the secret to repair work. It's definitely the first thing to check. Just one tiny bit of loose wire, and poof! Nothing works." She went to work replacing the wire, and failed to notice the strained expression on Brad's face.

"Yeah, well, the motor's important, too, you know," he said stubbornly. "Motors are complicated, and a lot can go wrong with them."

"Hey, Brad," Mitch called out. "Are you sleeping on the job or what?"

"What do you mean?" Brad said grumpily.

"He means that you've been standing around staring at the ceiling for the last half hour while Nora's been doing all the work." Tommy Ryder chuckled.

"Yeah, I thought you were supposed to be the master mechanic," Mitch teased him. "Or is Nora too much for you?"

Mr. Robino appeared just then, his round face creased in a broad smile. "Ah, nice work," he said, inspecting the fan. "I wondered when you two would get around to checking the wiring."

"It came to me in the middle of the night, Mr. Robino," Nora said excitedly. "I couldn't sleep, so I got up to read another chapter in my home appliance repair book."

"You got up in the middle of the night to read about appliance repair?" Mr. Robino teased her gently. "Such dedication! No wonder you have made so much progress."

"Well, I don't know about that," Nora said, flushing, "but they had this full-page drawing of an electrical system, and as soon as I saw it, I thought of the fan. I just *knew* that had to be the problem."

"Well, let's try the final test," Mr. Robino said, reaching for the plug. He plugged the fan into the wall, flipped a switch, and the blades began to spin. "You did it!" he congratulated her.

"*We* did it," Nora said quickly, but it was too late. The chubby little instructor had already moved on to another row.

"Nice work, Nora," Brad said sarcastically. "Whenever I want an expert on wiring, I'll know where to go." The bell rang then and he shrugged into his jacket and turned away, leaving Nora open-mouthed

"Uh-oh," Tracy said at Nora's elbow. "I think you blew it."

"I think so, too," Nora admitted through gritted teeth. It was just so unfair! She picked up her books slowly, replaying the scene in her mind. What could she have done differently?

Later that afternoon as they were walking home together, Nora asked Jen the same question.

"But you didn't do anything wrong!" Jen insisted, her green eyes serious. "Why should you have to apologize for being a good student? If Brad was any kind of friend at all, he'd be *proud* of you!"

"Unfortunately, things just don't seem to work that way — at least not with boys," Nora said ruefully. "Remember what Tracy said — that I'd have to play dumb if I wanted Brad to be interested in me? Well, I'm beginning to think she's right."

"Nora Ryan, that's the craziest thing I've ever heard, and you know it." Jen came to a complete stop and grabbed Nora's arm. "I'm not going to walk another step until you take that back!"

"Honestly, Jen," Nora said, laughing, "I didn't say I agreed with Tracy, or that I was going to follow her advice. I just said that maybe she has a point." Nora pulled up the hood on her friend's yellow rain slicker as a light drizzle started to fall. "C'mon, we're going to get soaked standing around here arguing."

She made a move, but Jen held back. "Do you promise not to ever say anything so insane again?"

"I promise," Nora said. I'll still go on thinking it though, she thought. The truth is that I made Brad look bad in front of his friends, and he's never, *ever* going to forgive me for it!

Chapter 6

"So you want to go to Washington?" Nora's father asked a couple of nights later. It was early evening, and he was stretched out in a tan leather lounge chair that the family had bought him last Christmas. "I think we can probably arrange that — unless you're planning on staying at the Ritz," he teased. He reached for his glasses and peered at the mimeographed sheets from Mr. Robards.

"The Ritz is in New York, Daddy," Nora said.

"The hotel doesn't cost much. Plus, we're staying four to a room. And we're eating some meals at a budget cafeteria," she added, in case he needed some extra convincing.

"Well, in that case," he said, laughing, "I think we can swing it." He signed his name with a flourish on the bottom of the page. "You, Nora Ryan, hereby have my permission to go to Washington, D.C., and do the town. How's that?"

"Terrific!" Nora kissed the top of his head. "Thanks, Daddy!"

"I remember the last time I was in Washington," Mr. Ryan began. "It was a number of years ago, of course, but I can see it like it was yesterday. It was early spring, in cherry blossom time. . . ." He pushed his glasses up on the top of his head — where his brown hair was thinning slightly, Nora noticed — and stretched out his long legs until his feet rested on the leather ottoman.

Oh no, Nora thought, her spirits sinking. When Dad gets started on a story, he's good for half an hour! Nora smiled politely as her father reminisced about his trip, and tried not to glance at the den clock. She'd promised to call Jen at eight sharp.

"The Air and Space Museum was definitely one of the highlights," her father said fondly, breaking into her thoughts. "Do you know they have a Sopwith Camel there?" When Nora looked blank, he went on: "That's a classic fighter plane from World War I. And there are Spitfires, and Mustangs, and ME 109s. . . . And you know something? They've even got Lindbergh's plane there. Can you imagine that?

What a fantastic place!" He shook his head and reached for his pipe. "I can remember talking to a British fighter pilot in the lobby one day. . . ."

A few minutes later, Jen's voice raced over the phone. "Well, what's the verdict?" she asked breathlessly.

"I'm going!" Nora said happily. Not that there was ever much doubt, she thought to herself. Her parents had always encouraged her to participate in extracurricular activities, and school trips were high on the list. She was sitting cross-legged on her bed, doing some easy "fill-in-the-blank" French homework, with the phone cupped under her chin.

"Me, too!" Jen cried. "I thought I'd die waiting for Dad to come home. He was stuck in some meeting or other and couldn't leave work until really late."

"So we're all set," Nora said thoughtfully. "Do you think they'll assign rooms, or can we choose our own roommates?" She paused. "I can think of half a dozen people that I *know* I don't want to be stuck with."

"Gosh, I know what you mean," Jen agreed. "Having the wrong roommates can really ruin a trip. Remember that time we went to camp together and Sandy Miller snored all night?"

"Give me a break," Nora moaned. "She said that she snored because she was sleeping on the top bunk."

"And no one would trade with her!" Jen chuckled.

There was a pause in the conversation while Nora started work on another sheet of French homework. "Does *aller* take *être* or *avoir*?"

"*Être*," Jen said, surprised. "I can't believe you're working on French verbs at a time like this," she protested. "Usually you get all your homework done by eight o'clock."

"I try to," Nora admitted. "But tonight I just got wrapped up in this new appliance book I bought, and — " Nora yawned and glanced at the clock. "Wow, it's later than I thought. I've still got three pages left, so maybe. . . ."

"Maybe we should continue this conversation tomorrow," Jen said dryly. "You want me to buzz off. I get the hint," she added with a mock sigh.

"Jen, I didn't mean to make you mad," Nora said quickly.

A bubbly laugh reassured her. "I'm not mad, I'm just teasing you. I promise to hang up right away, but first tell me what you're wearing tomorrow." This was a ritual Nora and Jen had gone through ever since they were little.

Nora squinted her eyes and stared at the ceiling. "My blue shirt with my new jeans — no wait, they're in the hamper. I'll have to wear the faded Lees. They're a little big around the waist, so I'm going to borrow Sally's new macrame belt."

"I'm wearing a yellow sweater — "

"Are you going to wear it backwards?" Nora asked with a chuckle.

"Backwards? Oh, I know what you mean." Jen laughed. "No, I've gotten off that kick. That was always more Denise's style than mine anyway."

"There's nothing *wrong* with that look," Nora said. "It's just that I always liked you better the way you are."

"I guess I do, too," Jen said happily. "I don't really like a lot of those way-out styles. . . . Of course Denise is so gorgeous, she can get away with anything." She paused. "Well, I guess I better let you get back to your French verbs."

Fifteen minutes later, Nora had finished the French homework and reached under the bed for Jen's copy of *Teen Beat*. She started to flip through to the article on Trilogy, when she noticed her home appliance book was still open on her night table. She'd been reading a fascinating chapter on electric fans before dinner, when she'd been called away to help her father set the table. She looked at the copy of *Teen Beat* in her hand and sighed. What a dilemma — she certainly didn't have time to read them both!

"I was so excited I could hardly sleep last night," Tracy Douglas said a week later at lunch.

"Me, too," Lucy Armanson piped up. "We were so noisy in homeroom that Ms. Osmond said we all must have a new disease: Washington fever." She poked at her cottage cheese salad without much enthusiasm. "It's going to seem like a million years between now and Friday."

"But there's so many things to do before we leave," Tracy protested. "I need to get my hair trimmed." She picked up a lock of shiny blonde hair and looked at it critically. "Just an eighth of an inch, though."

"An eighth of an inch!" Nora shook her head as she buttered a slice of whole wheat bread. "Tracy, you're too much. I've never seen anyone as hung up on their hair as you are."

"I'm not hung up," Tracy said in her little-girl voice. "It's just that my hair is my best feature." When Nora groaned, she glared at her. "Well, everyone says so!"

"Have it your way," Nora relented. "But I wish you'd believe me, Tracy. Everyone thinks you — and your hair — look great just the way you are. You don't need to worry about your looks every five minutes."

"Well, I don't know about that," Tracy said, glancing toward a long table in the back of the cafeteria where Mitch Pauley and Tommy Ryder were sitting. "I mean, it would be nice if the right people thought I looked great." She rolled her eyes dramatically toward the boys. "Know what I mean?"

"Yes, we do," Jen reassured her. Poor Tracy, she thought. Having a boy who likes her is the most important thing in the world to her!

"Who's going to room together?" Nora said. Always the practical one of the group, Nora liked to keep everyone organized. "Has anybody heard how Mr. Robards is going to handle room assignments?"

"It's first come, first served," Lucy said, pushing aside the rest of her cottage cheese. "He's going to post a list in his office today." She paused. "Gosh, what can I have for dessert that isn't fattening? I'm still starving," she said, glancing wistfully at the serving line.

When Nora tried to say something, Lucy laughed and held up her hand. "Please! I know how you feel about prune whip." She smiled and got up. "I think I'll pass this time."

"I'll split a piece of lemon pie with you," Tracy said, digging in her purse for some change.

"But that's fattening," Lucy objected.

"Yeah, but it's yummy, and besides, you earned it after eating that cottage cheese."

"I don't know . . ." Lucy said doubtfully.

"I do. Get a big piece," Tracy called, as Lucy headed for the line. "Do you guys want to room with me?" she said hopefully. "Lucy can be the fourth."

"Sure," Jen said quickly. "That would be great, wouldn't it, Nora? Let's ask Lucy as soon as she gets back."

"It's fine with me," Nora told her. "But let's make sure we get to Mr. Robards right after lunch and sign up."

"Just think," Tracy said dreamily, "this is going to be my first coed trip away from home. Talk about wall-to-wall guys!"

"Uh, Tracy, I wouldn't get my hopes up," Jen said. "Mr. Robards keeps the boys and girls on separate floors. There's not going to be too much partying going on."

"Oh!" Tracy said, making a face. "I thought maybe there'd be late-night pizza dates and things like that."

Nora and Jen exchanged a look.

"Tracy," Jen said firmly, "this trip is supposed to be educational. Believe me, you've got the wrong idea completely!"

"Dessert time!" Lucy said, sliding into her seat. "All the calories you could ever — " Whatever Lucy was about to say was lost in a gasp of surprise as a hand suddenly appeared from nowhere, and lifted the meringue topping from her pie. "Jason Anthony!" she yelled. "You . . . you — " she spluttered.

"Hmmm, delicious," Jason said, licking his fingers one by one. "My compliments to the chef," he said grandly. He was wearing a pea-soup green T-shirt that made his bright red hair seem more fiery than usual.

"Jason, you're such a. . . ." Tracy paused, rolling her big blue eyes. Words failed her.

"I'm waiting." Jason said, pretending to be taking notes as he started to scoot away. "I'm trying to learn twenty-five new vocabulary words a week."

He stepped out of reach and gave a deep bow, then darted across the grimy linoleum floor to the safety of the far wall.

"I could kill that kid," Lucy said. "I could actually *kill* him!"

"Forget him," Tracy advised. "He's not worth getting excited over."

"I'm not *excited*," Lucy insisted. "I'm

hungry and that little rat ruined my pie!"

Nora patted her arm sympathetically. "Don't be upset, Lucy," she said consolingly. "Jason did you a favor. Look over at the serving line."

"What do you mean?" Lucy asked, following Nora's gaze.

Nora gave a superior smile. "Didn't you notice? The cook just put out a whole new tray of prune whip — now's the perfect chance to try it!"

Chapter 7

The next few days passed in a blur of excitement, as Jen and Nora debated endlessly what to pack for the trip. Late Thursday night, Nora called Jen for a last-minute discussion.

"I'm just going down my checklist," Nora began, "and we need to go over a few things." She was curled up in bed, cozy in her red Dr. Denton's, with a yellow legal pad balanced on her knees.

"*Another* checklist?" Jen groaned. "I thought we covered everything last night."

"This is my *final* checklist," Nora said calmly. "The others were just preliminary ones."

"Okay, okay," Jen interrupted. She knew that it was impossible to rush Nora when she was in one of these moods.

"Well, music, for one thing," Nora said, chewing on the end of her felt-tipped pen.

"I'm bringing the tape player for the bus ride," she said, making a small check mark on the pad, "but shouldn't we each choose some tapes?"

"I guess so," Jen said. "I hadn't really thought about it." Since Nora and Jen had the same taste in music — and in practically everything else — they often traded tapes back and forth. In fact, sometimes it was hard to remember who actually owned what. "How about if you bring Mr. Mister, and I bring Power Station," Jen added.

"Sounds good." Nora made a small check mark on the list. "Okay, that leaves snacks for the trip."

"We could buy some on the way," Jen suggested. "Mr. Robards said we'll be making lots of stops."

"Jen, you can't be serious!" Nora said, outraged. "Eat Twinkies out of a machine? No, I mean *real* snacks, things like sunflower seeds and granola and dried pineapple."

"Whatever you say," Jen sighed. "I could ask Jeff to make those wheat-germ-and-molasses brownies you like." It was one of the few desserts that Nora actually approved of.

"That's more like it." Nora sounded pleased.

"And you're bringing mostly jeans, tops,

and a dress to wear for dinner?"

"Right. I'm wearing Nikes and borrowing a pair of low-heeled navy blue pumps from Sally. How about you?"

"The same," Jen said promptly. "Dad made me buy a pair of navy blue pumps last fall because they'd go with everything." She sighed. It was really hard going on shopping expeditions with her father, but it was even worse when he picked out clothes by himself. A few months ago, he'd "surprised" her with a yellow rain slicker that made her look about eight years old. She wondered if she should bring it. . . .

"What about raincoats?" Nora asked, as if she had read her mind.

"Gosh, I was just thinking about that. How about if I borrow that big black umbrella from Dad instead? We can both fit under it."

"Great." Nora paused and studied the list. "Are you excited about tomorrow?"

"I've got a stomachache," Jen admitted. She always felt edgy when she went on a trip, and except for a week at camp, she had never been away from her family.

Nora laughed. "It's just butterflies." She glanced at the clock. "Gosh, we better get some sleep. See you in . . . seven-and-a-half hours!"

"I won't sleep a wink," Jen moaned, as she hung up the phone.

"Jen, did you forget to set the alarm?" Eric's voice cut like a razor through his sister's sleep-fogged brain.

"Set the alarm . . ." Jen muttered. "Don't think so," she slurred, burrowing her face deeper in the pillow.

"You must have!" Eric yelled, pulling the covers off the bed. "Isn't today your school trip? Jeff's already got breakfast out for you."

"School trip — omigosh!" Jen squealed, jumping out of bed. Of all the mornings to oversleep! "What time is it?"

"Six-twenty."

"Oh no," Jen wailed. She looked frantically around the room for the faded jeans and yellow knit shirt she planned to wear that morning. "Tell Jeff I'll be right down."

Half an hour later, she arrived breathlessly at the Cedar Groves parking lot. A huge red-and-white bus was idling noisily at the curb, sending black exhaust fumes into the damp morning air, while Ms. Anderson took roll.

Mr. Robards was helping the driver tag luggage, and when he spotted Jen, he called, "Over here with your suitcase, Jen. We're leaving in three minutes."

Jen handed over her suitcase just as Nora caught up with her.

"Where *were* you!" Nora demanded. "I was just going to run inside and call your house!"

"I overslept," Jen admitted sheepishly. "Pretty silly, huh?"

"At least you made it," Nora said, pulling her toward the bus. "Quick, let's get in line so we can get good seats."

"I think the seats are all the same," Susan Hillard said in a bored voice. "Hard as a rock." She gave a long, theatrical sigh. "I wish we could have taken a plane instead." She looked enviously at Denise. "I'm surprised she didn't charter a Lear jet," she muttered to no one in particular.

Denise pretended not to hear her, and searched for her sunglasses.

"Oh, Susan, it won't be that bad. Try to make the best of it," Amy Williams said cheerfully. "You can pretend you're roughing it."

Denise giggled, and Amy turned to grin at her. Her eyes skimmed over Denise's outfit, and she recognized the bright red silk top — she had seen one just like it in the new *Vogue* magazine. And the black pants were exactly like the ones Cher had worn under a sari at a movie premiere last month. Only Denise would wear something like that, Amy thought. And only Denise could get away with it.

"I don't have to *pretend*," Susan said in a haughty tone. "Riding on a bus all day *is* roughing it!"

"Maybe you'd rather take a camel!" Jason Anthony hooted. He had come equipped with his skateboard, Nora noticed, and she wondered if Mr. Robards would confiscate it. I certainly hope so, she thought fervently. She could just picture Jason skateboarding up and down the steps of the Jefferson Memorial!

Susan glared at Jason and flounced over to the bus, just as the driver yelled, "Hey, are there two girls named Hendrix — or maybe three?"

"No, just one," Ms. Anderson called back. "Denise."

"Well, there's half a dozen pieces of luggage with the same name on it," the driver grumbled, hoisting a beautiful tan leather overnight bag under the bus.

"It's all mine," Denise said, unembarrassed. "I always pack a lot."

"Gosh," Tracy Douglas said in an awed tone.

"Okay, everybody," Ms. Anderson's voice cut through the babble of voices. She was a popular young teacher who wore her long auburn hair swept back in a ponytail and never wore anything on her feet except clogs. Today she was dressed casually in a pair of trim khaki pants and an oversized navy sweater. "Time's getting away from us, so let's hit the road!"

"I feel like I've been on this bus for hours," Lucy Armanson said much later that day. It was early afternoon and the bus was speeding through the rolling hillsides of western Virginia.

"You have," Tracy Douglas said, glancing at her watch. "We all have." She gingerly shifted her position, trying to straighten her cramped legs. The first couple of hours had been fun, but now that they'd listened to all the tapes and eaten all the snacks, there was nothing left to do! She stretched out her arm and accidentally elbowed Denise Hendrix in the ribs.

"Are we there yet?" Denise asked groggily. Denise had an amazing ability to sleep anywhere — probably because of all the traveling she did, Nora thought — and had been dead to the world since they left Cedar Groves.

"No," Tracy whispered.

Nora was staring out the window, daydreaming, and found herself thinking about Brad Hartley, who was sitting in front of her. If only he hadn't changed so much, she thought sadly. He never smiled or joked with her anymore. They just worked silently side by side, as if they hardly knew each other. Almost like they were strangers.

And Mr. Robino certainly wasn't making things any better. He kept saying over and over what an inspiration Nora was to the class, and that he'd never seen anyone make so much progress in so short a time. Every time he'd give Nora a compliment, Brad would start to fidget with a motor and pretend he wasn't listening. It didn't take an Einstein to see that he was jealous!

Of course, it was silly to blame Mr. Robino, Nora admitted glumly. What was it Tracy had said? "All you have to do is play dumb." Play dumb. Nora sighed and shook her head. If you had to play dumb to get a guy, how could he be worth having?

Later that night, when they had checked into the hotel and eaten dinner, Nora sat curled up in bed with her guidebook. She looked around the room approvingly — it was small, but comfortable with two double beds and a long dressing table that Tracy had already littered with an amazing number of cosmetics.

"I can't really believe you use all that stuff every night," Jen was saying in a horrified tone. She was sitting on the bottom of Nora's bed, wearing her favorite nightshirt.

"It's not that much," Tracy said surprised. "You know my cousin Sandra, the one who models in New York? She spends half an hour moisturizing her *feet* every night! Can you imagine that?" Tracy began rubbing a thick cream all over her face. "I just concentrate on the parts of me that show," she said in her soft voice.

"Omigosh!" Lucy Armanson said, coming out of the bathroom. She looked at Tracy and pretended to fall back on the bed in horror. *"Halloween, Part Two."*

"It's a deep-cleansing mask," Tracy said, grinning. When she smiled, the mask started cracking, giving her an even more bizarre appearance. "It gives your face a rosy glow, and a porcelain finish," she said seriously.

"Well, it almost gave me a heart attack," Lucy said, jumping up and flipping on the TV. "Who wants to watch the late show? They've got *The Return of the Thing* on tonight." She turned to Jen. "That's one of your favorites, isn't it?"

"It sure is," Nora laughed. "She's seen it five times."

"Six," Jen corrected her. "But I

wouldn't mind watching it again." She grabbed a pillow and propped it behind her. "I hate to be a party-pooper, but aren't we supposed to have lights out by eleven?"

"They won't be fussy the first night," Lucy said. "But just to be on the safe side, let's keep the volume down low. Is this okay for you, Nora?"

Nora waved her hand and went back to her magazine.

"She's still reading that Trilogy article," Jen explained. "I would have thought you'd have it memorized by now."

"No, I never got around to the last page," Nora said, and then she gasped in surprise. "Wow, I can't believe it!" she blurted out.

"What is it?" Lucy said, without turning around. The movie had started and the Thing was slithering under a doorway.

"It's just . . . such a coincidence," Nora said, sitting straight up in bed. "Trilogy is here!"

"They're here?" Tracy asked. She looked around the room, as if she expected the members of the rock group to jump out of the closet.

"Not *here*, silly," Nora said impatiently. "Here in Washington. They're giving a big concert on Sunday."

"Well, you know we can't go on Sunday,"

Tracy said reasonably. "First of all, we don't have tickets, and anyway, I think that's the day we go to Wolftrap."

"I know we can't go to the concert," Nora said. "I just meant it would be fantastic if we could meet them."

"How would we do that?"

Nora sighed. Tracy had no imagination at all. "I don't know," she said irritably. "Maybe we could run into them or something. Maybe we could find out where they're staying and try to get an autograph, or . . . well, I don't know," she said helplessly. "It was just an idea."

A commercial blared, and Lucy swung around to look at Nora. "Nora, I hate to tell you, but we have as much chance of running into Trilogy, as we do of running into the Thing!"

"I guess you're right," Nora said slowly. She adjusted the reading light and studied the picture of the group. Peter Marks, Michael Stevens, Terry Reggles, and Timothy Downs — it would be so terrific to meet them, if only for a split second!

She stared blankly at the television screen as the Thing claimed its third — or maybe its fourth — victim. Meeting Trilogy would be a fantasy, a dream come true. But Lucy was right — the whole idea was crazy!

Chapter 8

"What are we doing today?" Jen asked Nora the next morning, as they waited outside the hotel for the bus driver to appear.

"We've got a full schedule," Nora said, consulting her list. "We start with the Air and Space Museum, and then move on to the Museum of American History."

"I've heard of that. They've got Archie Bunker's chair there!" Tracy Douglas said excitedly.

"And they have the First Ladies' dresses — the ones they wore to the Inaugural Ball," Ms. Anderson volunteered.

"Let's grab those same seats in the back," Jen said in a low voice as the bus pulled up. "We'll be able to get a great view of the city when we go over the bridge."

"Sure, only...." Nora paused and did a

double take. She'd spotted a flash of spiked blond hair and a famous, finely chiseled profile, just a few yards away. A siren went off in her head — could it really be him? Of course, lots of boys wore their hair that way. . . . But still, there was something about the way the hair fell over one eye, and there was that same cute cleft in his chin. She shook her head and looked again. No, it was impossible. It couldn't be him, not here, not now!

"What's wrong?" Jen asked, concerned. Nora was opening and closing her mouth rapidly like a fish.

"Jen," Nora said breathlessly, "the blond guy getting into the limo, is that who I think it is?"

"Where? What blond guy?" Jen turned too late and caught a glimpse of a stretch limo with tinted windows pulling away from the curb.

"Nothing," Nora said, swallowing hard. "For one crazy minute, I thought. . . . No, never mind," she said, suddenly embarrassed.

"You thought what?" Jen said, interested.

"I thought I saw Peter Marks." She glanced around to make sure no one had overheard. They'd all think she was crazy!

"Peter Marks? You must be more tired

than I thought," Jen laughed. "You're hallucinating!"

"It must have been the light," Nora admitted. She wished she hadn't said anything. The whole idea was crazy.

"I think it was your *eyes*," Jen teased her. "Now, c'mon, let's get those seats!"

"Beautiful, absolutely breathtaking," Ms. Anderson said later that day. She was leading a group of girls through the First Ladies' Hall in the Museum of American History.

"Why is it so dark in here?" Mia Stevens said, annoyed. "I'm stumbling around like a bat."

"I think it's your sunglasses," Nora said gently. "That's why you're . . . um . . . bumping into things." She looked at Mia, who had layered a black-and-white checkerboard blouse and an aqua tank top over a pair of strawberry-colored pants.

"Yeah?" Mia took off her oversized black glasses and peered at the display cases. "It's *still* dark in here. They must be trying to save on the electric bill."

"No, that's not it," Ms. Anderson laughed. "They keep it dark so that the First Ladies' dresses don't deteriorate. The material is very fragile and some of it is very old."

"I'll say. Look at the get-up that Mrs. Lincoln wore."

Everyone turned to the mannequin in the somber black dress.

"Gosh," Tracy Douglas said, "she wore it to a New Year's Day reception in 1864."

"Hah! It must not have been much of a party. She looks like she's going to a funeral," Mia sniffed. "Not my style at all, even though it's total black."

"*Nobody* wore your style then, Mia," Susan Hillard said snidely. She stared at Mia's hair, which was spiked in popsicle shades of orange and hot pink.

Mia shrugged, unconcerned, and turned her attention back to the mannequins. "This is supposed to be a replica of the East Room of the White House," Ms. Anderson said, as they moved to another display window. The mannequins were posed in an elegant room filled with ornate furniture and heavy satin drapes.

"Oh, look at that one with all the fringe and sequins on her dress," Mia said suddenly. "She looks like one of those people out of the twenties. The ones who used to dance the Charleston — what do you call them, Ms. Anderson?"

"That's a little before my time," Jane Anderson said, smiling, "but I think you mean flappers." She paused and read the plaque. "Grace Coolidge."

"Sarah Childress Polk," Amy Williams said a few moments later. "Why does that name ring a bell?"

No one answered her for a moment, and then Nora snapped her fingers. "She put the first bathroom in the White House."

"Really!" Jen said, impressed. "Gosh, Nora, you're amazing. You've got a brain like an encyclopedia."

"I read it in a trivia book." Nora giggled as they moved on.

"I love that necklace," Denise said suddenly, pointing to a stylishly dressed mannequin in the next display room. "The pearl choker — it looks just like one that Princess Di wears."

"Maybe so, but Helen Taft wore it first," Ms. Anderson said. "Isn't it funny how fashions come back in style?"

Susan stole a look at Mia Steven's cotton-candy hair and neon-colored pants. "Some things are never *in* style," she muttered.

Nora was tired when they got back to the hotel, and flopped on the bed for a quick nap before dinner. Sleep was impossible, though, because a minute later, Jen, Tracy, and Lucy burst into the room, giggling loudly.

"I'm telling you, you're crazy, Jen," Lucy insisted. "The woman at the desk thinks you're nuts."

"She really does," Tracy said, nodding her blonde head up and down in agreement. "I'm warning you, Jen, if we see that same desk clerk on the way down to dinner, I'm going to pretend I'm not even *with* you."

"What's going on?" Nora said curiously.

"Our roommate is imagining things," Lucy said, pointing to Jen and tapping her head meaningfully.

"Seeing things that aren't there," Tracy said helpfully.

"I'm telling you, it's true." She sat Indian-style on the bed next to Nora. "There's no doubt about it."

Nora took one look at her flushed face, and knew it hadn't been a dream. "You saw him, too?" she asked breathlessly.

"I really did," Jen said, her voice shaky. "He looks just like his pictures. In fact, *better!*" She reached into her purse for a hairbrush and everything spilled out on the floor. "Look at me. I'm so nervous, I can't even think!" She scrambled on the floor until she found the brush, and scooped her long hair back into a ponytail. "Who'd ever think that Peter Marks would be staying right in this hotel? It's like a . . . a dream!"

"I know what it's like," Nora reminded her. "I saw him this morning, remember? And *you* told me I was crazy!"

"I'm sorry about that, Nora," Jen said apologetically. "It just seemed so incredible!"

Tracy and Lucy exchanged a look, and Tracy carefully shut the door. Then Lucy walked over to the bed, and said quietly, "Nora, are you trying to tell me that *you* saw Peter Marks, too?"

"I sure did," Nora grinned. "This morning, just as we were leaving the hotel." Her grin grew even wider when she saw the astonished look slowly creep over Lucy's face.

"Omigosh! Trilogy is here!" Tracy shouted, as the news suddenly dawned on her. "It's the chance of a lifetime. It's. . . ."

"It's a *secret*, so hush!" Lucy commanded, clapping her hand over Tracy's open mouth. She looked nervously at the closed door. "These walls are paper-thin. If anybody else finds out. . . ." She let the sentence trail off, and looked at Tracy meaningfully. "Understand?"

Tracy nodded her head vigorously, and Lucy released her. "I thought Jen was just imagining it," she said apologetically. "The woman at the desk said it wasn't him —"

"That doesn't matter," Nora said

briskly. Nora turned to Jen. "Where did you see him?"

"In the corner of the lobby," Jen told her. "But it was only for a split second." She paused and stared at her image in the mirror. "It's so funny to see a celebrity in person," she began. "You know, you're used to seeing them on TV, or in videos, or magazines. . . ."

"Jen, get to the point!" Nora pleaded. "Exactly what was he doing in the lobby?"

"Well, I think he was there by mistake," Jen said. "He was walking down that little hallway, the one that leads from the lobby to outside, and he took a right instead of a left."

"And ended up practically smack at the front desk," Nora said thoughtfully. "What happened then?"

"As soon as he realized where he was, he darted back down the hallway. But the woman at the desk saw him," Jen insisted. "I know she did, because she smiled right at him."

"But why did she deny it a minute later when you asked her?" Tracy said, puzzled.

"Because she *has* to," Jen explained. "She can't admit that Peter Marks is staying here. She'd probably lose her job!"

"That makes sense," Lucy agreed. "If it *was* Peter Marks — "

"Do you mean you doubt it?" Tracy cried. "It has to be him — both Nora and Jen saw him!"

"I know they *thought* they saw him," Lucy said soothingly. "But the question is, Even if he's really staying here, how does that affect us? What can we do about it?"

"What can we *do* about it!" Jen said in astonishment. "Well, that's easy — we can *meet* him!" As soon as the words were out of her mouth, she felt calmer. Of course. That was the answer. She and Nora would devise a plan, something clever, something simple, and the four of them would meet Peter Marks. And the rest of Trilogy, of course, if they were staying here, too.

"We're really going to do it?" Tracy shouted. She looked from Jen to Nora to Lucy.

"We sure are," Nora said thoughtfully. "How about you two?" she said, looking at Lucy. "Are you in with us?"

Lucy looked at Tracy, who nodded silently, her face pale with excitement. Then Lucy took a deep breath and grinned from ear to ear. "We're all in this together!"

Chapter 9

"The first thing we've got to do is check out that hallway," Nora said the next morning after breakfast. She looked at her watch. "The bus will be here in exactly fifteen minutes, so we have to move fast."

"What should we do?" Tracy asked. She was beginning to feel a little nervous about the whole project. The desk clerk — the same one who was on duty the night before — was giving them a suspicious look as they lingered in the lobby. Tracy just knew that she'd be around the desk in a few seconds and demand to know what they were up to. And then what? It wasn't a warm day, but her new blue sweater suddenly felt hot and clingy. She wasn't cut out to be a spy. Why didn't her friends realize that?

"Tracy, will you stop looking so guilty?"

Lucy Armanson pleaded. "You're going to blow the whole thing."

"Do I look guilty?" Tracy gulped. Her face was crimson, and she bit her lower lip nervously.

Lucy rolled her eyes and turned Tracy around so her back was to the desk. "Just keep facing this way, and keep an eye out for Ms. Anderson."

"Right," Nora agreed. "Try to look casual. I'll be back in a minute." Nora strolled across the lobby as if she had all the time in the world. She glanced in the gift shop, checked a poster advertising the luncheon special, and finally made her way down the mysterious hallway.

But then she drew a blank. It was just a long carpeted hallway with some elevators and vending machines. She was almost at the end of the corridor when a familiar voice made her jump.

"Aren't you a little out of your territory, Nora?" It was Mr. Robards, and he was staring at her with a puzzled expression.

"I was. . . ." Suddenly she remembered the vending machines. "I was just looking for. . . ." Her voice trailed off in confusion.

Nora took a quick, desperate glance up and down the hall. "For the elevator," she said brightly. She was so nervous the words came out in a squeak.

"Oh, well, you're in the wrong corridor," he said, his face relaxing. "You can't use this elevator to get to your room," he added, gesturing to the closed green doors.

"No?"

"Nope." He shook his head. "This is an express elevator — it bypasses all the floors and goes straight to the penthouse."

"The penthouse!" she warbled. She felt like jumping up and down, but she forced her voice to remain neutral. Of course! That was where Peter Marks would be staying! "I didn't know they had anything like that here."

"Oh yes. It's supposed to be very nice," Mr. Robards said. "Out of our league, of course." He chuckled. "I've heard it even has a patio and a jacuzzi. Oh well," he sighed, "maybe someday, when we're all rich and famous."

Nora smiled weakly. "Right," she said, joining in the joke. She could hardly wait to get away and tell the others about this! Peter Marks was in their reach after all.

"You wanted extra towels?" a large woman in a white uniform suddenly emerged from a door Nora hadn't noticed before. It was marked: HOUSEKEEPING.

"That's what I'm here for," Mr. Robards said agreeably. "They seem to have forgotten us this morning." He reached for the towels, and Nora decided to make her getaway.

"See you on the bus," she said as she darted off.

"Don't you see, it's a snap!" she whispered excitedly to Jen an hour later. They had stopped to look at the Hope diamond in the Museum of Natural History, and Nora managed to get Jen, Lucy, and Tracy off to one side. "All we have to do is get down that corridor and take the elevator straight up to the penthouse. No one else even knows it's there."

"But Mr. Robards did," Jen said, unconvinced. "Plus, what if he shows up there again?"

"He won't run out of towels *twice*." Nora was beginning to get impatient. Jen didn't seem to appreciate how much progress she'd made. She'd practically solved the whole problem herself while the other girls were hanging around the lobby, wondering what to do next.

"Why do they call it the Hope diamond?" Jason materialized next to them.

"Because it was purchased by Henry Thomas Hope," Nora said automatically.

"Oh yeah?" said Jason.

"Yeah." Nora paused and turned her back on Jason. "Now, what we need to do next — "

Lucy gave her a warning nudge, and she stopped in midsentence. Jason was still standing there, hanging onto Nora's every word.

"What do we need to do next?" Jason parroted.

Lucy and Nora exchanged a desperate look. Jason showed no sign of leaving. Oddly enough, he seemed to want their company!

"Jason," Lucy said, lowering her voice, "did you know they take the diamond out of the display case once a day and let people touch it?"

"No, I didn't." Jason looked impressed.

"Well, don't let it get around," Lucy said earnestly, "but they're going to be showing it in Gallery forty-eight in exactly five minutes."

"Gallery forty-eight?" Jason's eyes were wide with excitement. "Where's that?"

Lucy made a vague gesture. "Oh, you know, it's down by the North American Indian display, behind the Blue Whale exhibit. Just stay to the right when you pass Birds and Mammals, and take a left when you get to Seashells."

"Oh, sure," Jason said, looking a little

dazed. "Five minutes, huh? Thanks!" He rushed away excitedly, making Tracy laugh.

"That was mean," she said reproachfully.

"But necessary," Lucy said crisply. "We only have a few more minutes alone, and we've got a lot to talk about." The rest of the group had already moved on to the Mineral collection in the next room, and she knew that Ms. Anderson would reappear at any moment to collect them.

Nora nodded. "We don't dare talk about this on the bus. If word ever got out. . . ."

They spoke quietly for a few more minutes before Ms. Anderson stuck her head around the corner.

"I wondered where you girls were!" she called cheerfully. "You got caught up in all these fabulous gems, didn't you?"

"Something like that," Nora said, pretending to look at a pale blue ring.

They followed Ms. Anderson past a brilliantly colored display of American Indian jewelry, and on the way out, Tracy paused at an enormous crystal ball.

"Oh, I adore crystal balls," Ms. Anderson said girlishly. "And this one must be the biggest in the world. Look, it weighs over a hundred pounds and was cut in China," she said, reading from a small card. "Take a peek, and tell us what you see, Tracy. Maybe you can read the future."

Tracy peered dutifully into the ball and squinted her eyes.

"Well, what do you see?" Ms. Anderson asked.

"The ball is cloudy, but . . . wait! I see four girls," Tracy said in a mysterious voice, like a fortune-teller. "And the girls are very happy. . . ."

"Why are they happy?" Lucy asked, going along with the joke.

"They are happy, because they have just met someone special. . . . Someone they have always dreamed about."

"Ah, a tall dark stranger," Ms. Anderson kidded. "I should have known."

Tracy giggled, and looked up. "Actually, it was a tall *blond* one!"

"What's wrong with Jason Anthony?" Jen said when they came back from lunch that day. They had gone up to their room for a few minutes to freshen their makeup, and Lucy decided to grab an umbrella. The sky was dark and threatening, and she just knew she'd be caught on the Mall between museums and get soaked!

"Hah! You mean, what's *right* with Jason Anthony," Lucy said sarcastically.

"No, I'm serious," Jen said. "Haven't you noticed that he seemed down in the dumps this morning? He tagged along with Mr. Robards to the Air and Space Museum, but his heart just wasn't in it. And he didn't even try to get even for that diamond trick!" She slipped a red crew neck sweater on over her white blouse and faded jeans.

"I think you're right," Tracy said suddenly. "It's funny that we haven't seen him on his skateboard — not once! And I heard Mitch Pauley say that he didn't even want to go roller-skating with the rest of the guys last night. He just sat alone in the lobby and read a book!"

"So what? I don't know why you're worried about him," Lucy said in a bored voice. "As far as I'm concerned, it's a *pleasure* not to be bothered with him!"

"Maybe," Jen said doubtfully, "but I still think that — " She broke off in surprise when Nora burst into the room.

"It didn't work!" Nora said.

"What happened?" Lucy asked.

Nora grinned sheepishly. "I wanted to surprise you, so I decided to check out that elevator. The one that goes straight up to the penthouse."

"And" — Tracy jumped up from the bed — "did you get up there?"

"I couldn't even get the *door* to open," Nora admitted. "You need a key!"

"A key?" Tracy said blankly. "Why would you need a key for an elevator?"

"Think about it," Lucy said wryly.

There was a moment's silence, and then Tracy said slowly, "Oh, because if you didn't need a key, then *everybody* would be going up there."

"Exactly." Lucy sighed and turned to Nora. "Well, now what?"

"I don't know," Nora said. "We'll have to rethink this whole project. There *must* be another way to get up there — we'll just have to find it." She was going to say more, when a light tap on the door made her jump.

"The bus is here for the FBI tour!" Ms. Anderson called cheerily.

"Be right there," Nora yelled back. She looked at her three coconspirators and put her finger to her lips. "Not a word about Peter Marks to anyone," she warned. "Remember, not a word."

Tracy nodded solemnly. "My lips are sealed."

The idea came to Nora that night at dinner. Mr. Robards and Ms. Anderson were taking them to a concert at Wolftrap that evening, and they were having a quick supper at the Brooklyn Sub Shop next door to the hotel.

"This is fun, isn't it?" Jen said, munching on a tomato and sprouts hoagie with extra cheese.

Lucy looked at her curiously. "Yeah, but you're not eating the real thing," she pointed out. "You've got to have salami to have a real sub sandwich — and lots of onions and peppers." She reached for a napkin. "That's the way they make them in Philadelphia. I know because my sister lives there."

"I like it better just with vegetables," Jen insisted.

"So Jen has invented the first vegetarian sub," Nora said absently.

"Lots of people eat vegetarian subs," Jen pointed out. "A lot of rock stars are vegans, and I remember reading that — "

Nora's eyes opened wide and she nearly dropped her sandwich. "Say that again!" she commanded.

Jen looked startled. "I just said that a lot of rock stars are vegans," she began slowly. "It just means that they don't eat meat or dairy products."

"But what about Peter Marks? Isn't he a vegetarian, or whatever you call it, a vegan?" Nora said excitedly.

"As a matter of fact, he is," Jen said

thoughtfully. "It mentioned something about it in that Trilogy article. He said that he has a hard time getting food when he's on tour. They don't dare go to a restaurant because they'd be mobbed, so they always order their meals sent to the room."

"Then that's it — that's the key!" Nora said delightedly. "We've got it made!" Some kids sitting at the next booth turned around to stare at her, and she lowered her voice.

"The key to what?" Tracy asked. She'd read the article they were talking about, and she didn't see why they were getting so excited. Who cared if Peter Marks ate soybeans?

"The key to Trilogy," Nora said. She looked around the table, and Lucy was the first to catch on. She gave a little gasp of surprise and nodded her head.

"Think about it," Nora continued. "They must order food in all the time, right? Okay, so that means nobody would be suspicious if someone just . . . *appeared* with sub sandwiches for them." She glanced up at the waitress, who was wearing a red-and-white striped apron and a jaunty little hat. "Especially if that someone looked like a *real* waitress, from a *real* sub shop." She giggled. "And was holding a *real* sandwich, of course."

"You're right!" Lucy said. "It's perfect." She turned to Tracy. "Don't you get it? If Trilogy won't come to us — a sub sandwich will go to them!"

Tracy spoke slowly. "One of us is going to dress up as a waitress and deliver a sub sandwich to Peter Marks?" She felt terrified just thinking about the idea. It was crazy — they would never, *ever* get away with it!

"That's it," Lucy said happily. She put her thumb and forefinger together in an "Okay" sign to Nora. "What a fantastic idea! It's brilliant!"

"It's a winner," Jen said, her green eyes glowing.

"I know it will work," Nora added calmly. "All we need is careful planning and a little luck." She took another bite of her sandwich and looked expectantly at Tracy. "Well, Tracy, what do you think?"

"It's scary," Tracy said in a little voice.

Lucy nudged her and laughed. "Of course it's scary. That's what makes it so much fun!"

Chapter 10

"Gosh, can you believe it?" Amy Williams said in an amazed tone. "He eats eighteen hours a day!" It was late afternoon, and the group was standing in front of an eight-ton bull elephant in the Museum of Natural History.

"You mean he *used* to eat eighteen hours a day," Jen said wryly. "At the moment, he happens to be dead." She looked at the hairy animal and felt a shiver of revulsion mixed with sympathy. Why did people have to kill animals and stuff them? she wondered.

Jason Anthony was standing next to them, listening to a recorded message on a white telephone. He started to replace the receiver when Nora stopped him.

"Can I listen?"

"Sure," he said, handing her the phone. "The tape will start again in a minute. But hold it away from your ear, Nora. There are some elephant screeches right at the beginning that will blast you across the room."

Nora looked at him in surprise and gingerly picked up the receiver. "Thanks," she said, as he moved away. She held the phone a few inches from her ear, and winced when a series of loud squawks blared out from the receiver.

"He was telling the truth," Lucy Armanson said in surprise. "I can't believe it. The kid must be sick."

"Why do you say that?" Ms. Anderson asked. Her eyes followed Jason as he wandered over to a stuffed Indian tiger near the gift shop. He was staring blankly with his hands on the railing, looking listless and depressed.

"Because he's not himself," Lucy said, shaking her head.

"Maybe he's been replaced by an android," Mia Stevens suggested. She hummed a few bars from the theme music to *The Twilight Zone*.

"No, you know what I mean," Lucy laughed. "What he just did to Nora was completely out of character. The old Jason — the one we all know and love — would never have warned Nora about the noise. Never! In fact, he would have loved to see her burst an eardrum — then he could roll around the floor, laughing his head off."

"I think you're being a little too hard on him," Ms. Anderson said gently.

"No way," Susan Hillard said flatly. "You may know a lot about social science, Ms. Anderson, but you've never come across anything like Jason Anthony." She paused to glare at Jason. "He's a true social misfit."

The rest of the Museum of Natural History visit was a blur to Nora; she was too caught up in her plan to meet Peter Marks to really appreciate the floors of exhibits. She went over the details a dozen times in her mind, and decided the plan was almost foolproof.

There were a few minor snags of course — what if she couldn't borrow a waitress uniform? — and she was mulling them over when she bumped into Brad Hartley. He was in the dinosaur room, looking at the remains of a seven-ton creature called triceratops. The animal towered above them, its massive bones supported on a metal frame.

"I think I met him in a nightmare once," Nora said, hoping for a smile. "Or maybe it was *The Late Show*." She hadn't seen much of Brad on the trip, and she wondered how he would react to her. Maybe now that we aren't in shop class, he'll be a little friendlier, she thought.

Unfortunately, Brad's attitude hadn't changed. He nodded coolly and went back to reading the plaque. Not even a smile!

"It's amazing that they can reconstruct these things from tons of bones, isn't it?" Nora said quietly. Dead silence. She was beginning to feel like an idiot, talking to herself, when Brad finally turned to her. He looked as handsome as ever, she couldn't help noticing, in crisp khaki pants and a pale blue shirt.

"Some of the bones aren't real," he pointed out. "They look like they must be plaster of paris. I guess they couldn't find all of the original ones, so they had to make a few substitutions."

Nora nodded enthusiastically. Anything to get him talking! "You know what it reminds me of? A giant jigsaw puzzle."

"A puzzle with some of the pieces missing . . ." Brad said thoughtfully. They moved on to another exhibit showing an archaeological dig and some dinosaur footprints.

"And you don't even know what the picture is supposed to look like!" Nora pointed to a huge bird-dinosaur with a giant wingspread that hovered near the ceiling. "Look at the pteryodactl — who'd ever believe that it was real?"

"Who'd ever *want* to!" Brad joked.

Nora breathed a sigh of relief. Things were going better than she had hoped.

"I guess the dinosaurs just couldn't survive when people came along," Brad said, inspecting a giant tooth fossil. It was a dirty white color, and the size of a small baseball bat.

"That's not what did them in," Nora said. "Anyway, people and dinosaurs didn't even exist at the same time — that just happens on *The Flintstones*."

Mr. Robards, who had come up beside them, grinned and applauded. "Very good, Nora. Go on."

"There are a lot of theories about it," she hedged, trying not to look at Brad. Out of the corner of her eye she caught a glimpse of his face; it looked like a thundercloud.

"But what do *you* think?" Mr. Robards insisted.

Nora took a deep breath. "I think that the theory about the geological catastrophe is the right one."

Somewhere behind her, she heard Mitch Pauley snicker. "Yeah, I was just going to say the same thing." He hooted, and got a big laugh. "Isn't that right, Tommy?" He nudged Tommy Ryder, who was standing next to him, in the ribs.

Mr. Robards started a discussion of fossils and Nora relaxed a little. She was off the hook. She started to look for Brad, but he was heading for the next room with Mitch Pauley and Tommy Ryder in hot pursuit. Nora's spirits sank down somewhere around her ankles. She'd done it again! she thought miserably.

"I can only let you have it for half an hour," Jamie, the blonde waitress at the Brooklyn Sub Shop, was saying worriedly. "My boss gets in at six-thirty, and she'll kill me if she sees me out of uniform."

It was ten of six that night, and Nora, Jen, and Tracy were standing in the back of the sub shop, stuffing the red-and-white striped apron into a shopping bag.

"I promise you, you'll get it back. And we need the hat," Nora said, plucking a tiny red cap off the girl's head.

"Are you *sure* you can get me Peter Marks's autograph?" Jamie asked for the dozenth time.

"Of course, we're sure," Lucy said heartily. "And maybe even an autographed picture."

"Oh, that would be fantastic!" Jamie's face was glowing. "I wish I had known you were going to do this — I've got this gorgeous poster of him at home, and he could have signed it for me." She turned to Tracy. "You know the one. He's sitting on a black motorcycle, and he's got his guitar strapped on the back. . . ."

Lucy glanced at her watch. Everything was timed to the minute, and they had to get out of the sub shop right now! "Do you have the sandwiches ready?" she asked.

"I've got them right here." Jamie reached under the counter and handed Lucy a slightly greasy paper bag. "I'm afraid I used too much olive oil on the subs; they leaked a little."

"Don't worry about it," Lucy said, desperate to leave. "You made four of them, right?"

"Right," Jamie said in a dreamy voice. "One for each guy in Trilogy." She paused. "But I only charged you for three," she whispered.

"Thanks." Nora smiled at her.

"That's okay, I made them kind of small."

"No problem." Nora nodded to Tracy and Lucy and headed for the door. "Let's go!"

"I sure wish I was going with you," Jamie said wistfully, following them to the front of the shop. "But I couldn't get any-body to cover for me tonight."

"We'll be back before you know it," Tracy promised.

They were almost out the door when Jamie's hoarse voice stopped them.

"Remember, I want him to write some-thing special — something *personal*," she pleaded.

"I'll remember," Nora said between gritted teeth. They were halfway through the revolving door when Jamie's voice assaulted them again. "To Jamie, the most exciting girl I've ever met."

The four girls hurried back to the hotel and were just about to dash inside when Nora turned white. "Hold it!" she hissed. She came to a dead stop, and Tracy nearly tumbled over her.

"What's wrong?" Lucy said nervously.

"Mr. Robards is in the lobby and he's coming this way!" Nora flattened herself against the building and her friends lined up next to her.

"Oh no!" Tracy moaned. "I knew some-thing would go wrong, I just knew it. We weren't supposed to leave the hotel! What are we going to do?"

"Just stay calm," Lucy said firmly. "He'll never suspect anything is wrong — unless you tell him."

"I'm not going to tell him!" Tracy said indignantly.

"She means, unless you act frightened," Jen explained, just as the teacher came through the door.

"Hi, girls," Mr. Robards said cheerfully. "What are you up to?"

Oh no! He knows! Tracy thought. "Up to?" she babbled.

Mr. Robards gave Tracy a curious look, and Lucy jabbed her friend hard in the ribs.

"We're . . . we're not up to anything," she gasped. "We're . . . just shopping." Tracy leaned back against the building, as if she were going to collapse at any moment.

"Shopping?" Mr. Robards frowned.

"We *were* shopping," Nora explained. "In the hotel gift shop, and then we came out for a breath of air."

"Oh, I guess we can bend the rules just this once," he said. "But don't leave the hotel again without permission, okay?"

"We won't," Nora said. She held her breath, willing him to move on. At last he did.

Chapter 11

"Brooklyn Subs for the penthouse," Nora said to the bored-looking desk clerk in the hotel lobby. She tried to keep her voice casual, but her heart was beating like a tom-tom in her chest, and her stomach was churning.

"For the penthouse?" The small, red-haired receptionist frowned. "I'll have to — just a minute," she said as the telephone jangled. She cradled the phone on her shoulder and began to write furiously on a memo pad.

Hurry up, hurry up! Nora pleaded silently. She took a nervous peek around the hotel lobby. Thank goodness there was no sign of Mr. Robards or Ms. Anderson ... how would she ever explain what she was doing? One look at the butcher block apron and the ridiculous red cap and the whole game would be up! She stopped to tie her shoe and risked a quick look over her shoulder. She knew that Jen and Lucy were close by, and she thought she recognized the tips of Tracy's white Reeboks sticking out from behind a marble pillar.

"You want eight doubles for the fifth?" the desk clerk was saying in a whiny voice. "I can let you have them, but only until the ninth."

"Please, could I . . ." Nora began, but the desk clerk waved her hand impatiently. Nora nodded and fell silent, watching the big clock over the front entrance. In just a few minutes, everyone would meet in the lobby to go to dinner. In fact, for all she knew, Ms. Anderson could be in the elevator right this moment, heading downstairs, ready to meet the group. And when she saw Nora dressed up as a waitress —

"Now what were you saying?" Nora was jolted back to the present when she realized the desk clerk was staring at her.

"I — I," she stammered. "Subs for the penthouse!" she blurted out, holding up the grease-stained bag.

The clerk gave a long sigh and checked a register. "Okay, just leave them on the counter, and I'll have someone take them up when I get a chance."

"They have to go up *now*," Nora hissed. She leaned across the counter and smiled like a conspirator. "Peter Marks said the last ones were cold, and was he ever mad!"

The desk clerk's eyes flickered with interest. "Really?" she grinned at Nora. "I've heard he has a terrible temper, but he's always been pretty nice to us. What did he order this time?" she said, peering at the bag.

"His favorite," Nora said promptly. "Soybean mush on alfalfa sprouts. And look," she said sternly, "if they're cold again, I'm going to be in a lot of trouble."

The girl stared at her for a moment and then shrugged. "Okay, I'll take them up right away. *Nobody* should have to eat that stuff *cold*," she giggled. "I'll make sure he gets them," she said, reaching for the bag.

Nora was desperately trying to think of a new argument when a hearty voice boomed across the lobby. "Stay here, everyone, while I sign us in and get the room keys. And don't forget, the bus leaves at seven sharp for dinner at Pete's Ribs!" A large man in a navy blue suit was making his way steadily to the front desk, through a group of noisy camera-laden visitors.

"Oh no," the desk clerk said softly. "It can't be true! Clements tours! Forty-four people and they're here a day early!"

Her face started to crumple and Nora decided this was the time to press her advantage. "The subs," she said quickly. "Just give me the elevator key, and I'll — "

The desk clerk didn't even hesitate. "Just this once," she whispered. "It's the first elevator down the corridor by the gift shop. Bellboy!" she shouted as a mountain of luggage started to build in the lobby.

Nora grabbed the key just as the main elevator doors opened and a bunch of her classmates spilled into the lobby. She ducked her head and half ran to the corridor by the gift shop, nearly colliding with Jen, Tracy, and Lucy.

"What took so long?" Tracy wailed. "You were standing at the desk forever!"

"Did you get the key?" Lucy said eagerly. All three girls were huddled flat against the wall, where they couldn't be seen from the lobby.

"I got it!" Nora said breathlessly. "But it was close . . . very close. If that tour group hadn't come in just then. . . ." She gave a little shiver.

"Well never mind, at least you made it," Jen said. She took the key out of Nora's trembling fingers and fitted it into the lock. "Let's hope it works."

The elevator door sprang open, and they tumbled inside.

"So far, so good," Jen said, pressing the

button marked: PENTHOUSE. "Everything's going perfectly."

"Then why am I so nervous?" Nora said between chattering teeth. She suddenly felt like the whole project was crazy, doomed to failure. What in the world were they doing!

Moments later, Nora found herself outside a massive door labeled 1401. She glanced back toward the elevators where her friends were waiting. "Is this it?" she mouthed, pointing to the closed door.

Lucy shot her an exasperated look, and she realized how silly the question was. Of course this was it — it was the only door on the floor!

She knocked lightly on the door, rehearsing her opening words. From inside, she was sure she heard the sound of a steady drum beat. It sounded vaguely familiar, and she wondered if it was from Trilogy's newest single, "Never Leave Me."

A long moment passed, and suddenly the door swung open. Nora instinctively shut her eyes, her heart pounding, and when she opened them, she was face to face with a short, bald man wearing a pair of jeans and a faded T-shirt. He looked at her curiously, while she stammered out her speech.

"Brooklyn Subs — for Trilogy," she warbled.

He stared at her silently, and then yelled to someone in the suite. "Hey, did Peter order subs? I thought we were getting Chinese food tonight."

He opened the door a few inches wider, and Nora strained to see inside. The music was really quite loud, she noticed, but it was early Beatles, not Trilogy, after all. "Wait here a minute," he said. The bald man crossed the room, threw open another door, and ducked back when a cloud of steam billowed out. "Hey, Pete!" he yelled over the sound of running water. "Did you order subs?"

Ohhhh! Nora thought, her heart in her throat. It's Peter Marks and he's in the shower! She took a step over the threshold, hoping to hear that famous voice. Just wait till the girls hear about this, she thought. Everyone will die of shock! Before she had time to plan her next move, the little man was back at her side.

"He doesn't remember ordering them," he said apologetically, "but we'll take them, anyway. What do I owe you?"

"Uh . . . uh. . . ." Nora swallowed hard, her eyes sweeping the luxurious suite. She wanted to remember every single detail to tell her friends. "That will be, uh . . . six . . . six dollars," she said finally, wishing she could think of some way to prolong the conversation. If only Peter Marks would come out of the shower!

"Here's a ten, honey," the man said, passing her a bill.

"I don't have any . . ." she began, handing him the bag.

"That's okay." He smiled at her. "Keep the change."

And then the door swung softly shut.

"That's it?" Lucy said incredulously. "You didn't even *see* Peter Marks, or talk to him? You didn't see *any* of the guys in Trilogy?" It was twenty minutes later, and the four girls were huddled together on the bus, going to dinner.

"I told you everything that happened," Nora said patiently.

"But didn't Peter Marks say anything?" Tracy wailed. "He must have said *something* to the man who opened the door. You said he asked him if he ordered the subs," she pointed out.

"I think I heard Peter Marks say one word," Nora said thoughtfully. This was really stretching the truth quite a bit, but Tracy looked so disappointed that Nora wanted to say something to cheer her up.

"Really!" Jen asked with excitement. "What was it?"

"He said . . . 'what.' "

" 'What?' " Jen frowned. "That's all he said?"

"Well, it's better than nothing," Tracy piped up. "How did he say it?" she asked dreamily.

Nora squinted her eyes. She *had* heard a vague mumbling from the shower, and she decided to improvise. "His voice was low and husky," she said finally. "Really deep, you know, and of course, the shower made a lot of noise."

"Ooh," Tracy said softly, "I bet he sounded just like he did on 'You're Mine.' "

Nora smiled. "Yes, that's it. He sounded exactly like that."

There was a long pause, and then Lucy said, "You're sure there's nothing else that happened?"

"No, nothing," Nora said innocently. "I've told you everything there is." But deep down, she knew she wasn't telling the truth. Her fingers dug deep into her jeans pocket where she had stashed a roll she'd taken off a room service tray. Not just *any* room service tray, but the one that had been left right outside the door to the suite. Trilogy's room service tray. It *had* to be theirs, she reasoned — they'd taken over the whole penthouse! So that meant she owned a roll that had been *nibbled* on by ... whom? Peter Marks or maybe Michael Stevens or Terry Reggles. She nearly giggled with pleasure just thinking about it. She'd tell the girls about it later, of course, but for now, it was *her* secret!

"I've always loved Mount Vernon," Ms. Anderson was saying the following morning. "And I think you will, too." She was driving a slightly battered white rental van down the George Washington Memorial Parkway, carefully weaving her way in and out of the rush-hour traffic.

"It was George Washington's home, right?" Brad Hartley asked. He was sitting in the middle section of the van, flanked by Tommy Ryder and Mitch Pauley.

"That's right," Ms. Anderson said. She changed lanes suddenly and a trucker blasted her with his horn.

Nora put her head back against the seat and let the breeze wash over her. It was going to be a long day, she decided, and she was glad she'd chosen her most comfortable sneakers to wear with her jeans.

Only eight people had elected to go with Ms. Anderson to Mount Vernon; the rest of the kids were visiting the National

Gallery of Art and the Folger Shakespeare Library with Mr. Robards.

"That's funny," Ms. Anderson said suddenly. "We seem to be going slower and slower.... Look, everyone's passing us."

"Step on the gas," Tommy Ryder offered.

"She's already doing that," Mitch Pauley spoke up. He leaned over the seat and peered at the dials. "Hey, Ms. Anderson, did you notice that the temperature gauge is way over in the red? That means we're overheated. I know, because the same thing happened to my uncle on the Jersey Turnpike."

"Oh no," Ms. Anderson muttered, steering the van onto the shoulder. It was moving at a snail's pace, and she had difficulty with the steering. "This is all I need...."

"It was a real mess," Mitch said, clearly pleased at having something to contribute. "We were stuck there for *hours*, waiting for the motor to cool down. And you know how they say bad news comes in threes? Well, then this is the really funny part," he chortled. "When Uncle Ned pulled off the road, he ran over some broken glass and got a flat."

"So what was the third?" Tracy Douglas asked, interested.

"What?" Mitch said, looking a little annoyed.

"What was the third piece of bad news?" she repeated. She ticked off the items on her fingers. "The car overheating was one, and the flat was two, so what was the third?"

Mitch glared at her. "I dunno," he said finally.

"Please, everybody," Ms. Anderson said in a worried voice, "just be quiet so I can figure out what to do." They were stopped on a bed of gravel lining the parkway, and a steady stream of traffic whizzed by them.

"I can take a look under the hood," Brad Hartley offered. "I'm pretty good at tinkering with motors."

"Would you?" Ms. Anderson said gratefully. She opened her door and stepped out of the van. "That would be great, but be careful," she warned. "And everyone else," she added, sticking her head through the open window, "just stay put."

Chapter 12

"I don't think he's got the slightest idea how to fix it," Jen whispered to Nora. Nora nodded, watching Brad and Ms. Anderson having a worried conversation in front of the open hood of the van. Fifteen minutes had passed, and they seemed no closer to a solution than when Ms. Anderson had first pulled off the parkway. After checking the oil and the water, and tinkering with a few stray wires, Brad had scratched his head and stared hopelessly at the overheated engine.

"Why doesn't he *do* something!" Tracy said impatiently. "It must be a hundred degrees in this crummy van, and look at my hair," she wailed, pulling a lock of blonde curls in front of her nose. "It's frizzing up!" she said in horror. "My hair can't take humidity."

"Your hair's fine," Jen said soothingly.

She shifted uncomfortably on the hard vinyl seat. She glanced at Nora, who was staring at the hood with a thoughtful expression on her face.

"It's just like the VW," Nora said, half aloud.

"What is?" Jen asked.

"The same thing happened with Sally's boyfriend's car. Every time it was hot out, it overheated, and we had to go through a whole routine to get it started again."

"You mean you know what to do?" Jen said quietly.

Nora shrugged. "I guess I could give it a try, but. . . ." She nodded at Brad who was busily tying a white handkerchief on the door handle of the van. How can this be happening with Brad again? she mourned silently.

Jen followed her gaze and understood instantly. "You're worried about Brad, aren't you?" Jen said, keeping her voice low.

Nora was about to answer when Ms. Anderson opened the side door to the van. "We may as well get a little air in here," she said wearily. "It looks like we're going to be stuck here for a while."

"What's going to happen now?" Tracy asked, twisting a curl nervously around her finger.

"We just have to wait for a tow truck, I guess," Ms. Anderson said with a sigh. "Our only hope is that someone will see the handkerchief and take the time to call the state police."

"That could take hours!" Tracy cried.

"It certainly could," Ms. Anderson said grimly. "But unless we have a mechanical genius hiding in the backseat, there's not much else we can do."

Jen nudged Nora. "C'mon, tell her!" she pleaded.

Nora hesitated. "I don't know. . . ."

"Nora, please — this is an emergency!" Jen insisted. "Just tell Ms. Anderson you want to take a look under the hood. It can't hurt, and maybe you can fix it."

"Do you know how to fix the van?" Tracy said, leaning forward eagerly.

"I've . . . um . . . been in a situation like this before," Nora hedged.

"Well, then what are you waiting for? Do something!" Tracy begged.

"I thought I was supposed to act dumb around machinery," Nora hissed, glancing out the open window at Brad. "You said that was the way to get Brad's attention."

"Nora, forget what I said!" Tracy's voice rose to a squeal. "This is an emergency! I'm turning into a fuzzball!"

A couple of minutes later, Nora was peering into the depths of a grimy motor. "It's just like Greg Morton's," she said delightedly.

"Greg Morton?" Ms. Anderson looked blank.

"My sister's boyfriend," Nora explained. "His VW used to overheat all the time. Greg finally developed a foolproof way of fixing it."

"Do you think you can do it?" Ms. Anderson asked breathlessly.

"Well, I watched him do it plenty of times. Let's give it a try," she said, reaching for the radiator cap. "Now, if you'll just hand me that bottle of ice water."

Ten minutes later, Ms. Anderson turned the key and the motor gave a satisfying roar. "That's it!" she hooted triumphantly. "Let's hear it for Nora!"

A cheer went up from the occupants of the van, and Nora gave a shy smile as they headed back on the parkway.

"Way to go!" Tracy congratulated her, and even Mitch Pauley and Tommy Ryder looked properly impressed.

The biggest thrill of all, though, was when Brad Hartley turned around to face her. His eyes met hers for a long moment and he looked almost shamefaced. Then he smiled and winked at her. "Fantastic," he said softly. "Just fantastic."

"Nora, I'm sorry to interrupt your dinner, but can I see you for a moment?" Ms. Anderson's face was drawn as she tapped Nora on the shoulder that evening. They were having an early dinner at Little Joe's, a tiny Italian restaurant around the corner from the hotel. Ms. Anderson tried to smile reassuringly at the other students crowded into the booth, but the catch in her voice gave her away.

"Sure," Nora said, wriggling out of the red vinyl seat. Everyone stopped eating and stared at her as she followed Ms. Anderson to the front of the pizzeria, where Mr. Robards was waiting.

From the look on his face, it was obvious that something was very wrong. "Nora," he said abruptly, "when's the last time you saw Jason Anthony?"

"Jason?" Nora frowned and tried to think. "I guess it was today . . . at breakfast. He didn't come with us to Mt. Vernon, so I figured he spent the day with you, on the Mall. She stopped suddenly, as the truth slowly dawned on her. "Isn't he here tonight?"

Mr. Robards' face was grim. "Unfortunately not," he said. He glanced at Ms. Anderson. "We seem to have gotten our signals crossed. I thought he was going to Mt. Vernon with you, and Ms. Anderson thought he was with us."

"Do you mean he's —" Nora could hardly bring herself to say the word.

"Missing," Mr. Robards said flatly. "Probably since this morning. Nora, is there anything you can tell us about this? Do you have any idea what's wrong with Jason, or where he could be?"

"No," she said slowly. "I guess he seemed a little quiet on the trip . . . not like himself."

"I noticed that, too," Ms. Anderson said. "I should have talked to him about it."

"Don't worry about that now," Mr. Robards said. "The thing we have to do is concentrate on finding him."

"Could I help?" Nora offered. "Jen and I could check the hotel. . . ."

"We've already alerted the hotel. The desk clerk is going to be on the lookout for him, and he'll tell us if Jason shows up in the lobby." He gave a thin smile. "This may turn out to be nothing, you know. If we're lucky, Jason may have just stepped out to buy a candy bar or a magazine, and missed going with us this morning. He could turn up at any second."

"If we're lucky," Ms. Anderson said.

By seven o'clock that evening, it was apparent that Jason was nowhere in the hotel. Word of his disappearance had spread through the group, and reactions ranged from shock to disbelief.

"I think it's all a joke," Mitch Pauley said to Tommy Ryder in the lobby after dinner. "You know Jason — he'll probably pop out of a doorway with a big grin on his face and say, 'Gotcha!' "

"I don't think so," Steve Crowley said slowly. "This would be a pretty crazy stunt for someone — even Jason — to pull. Have you noticed how worried Mr. Robards and Ms. Anderson are? They've been pacing the floor for the last half hour."

"Yeah, I think you're right...." Tommy paused. "It's funny that he took his suitcase, though. I guess it could be part of a gag," he said thoughtfully.

"He took his suitcase?" Jen broke in. She was balanced on the edge of a sofa, watching television, half listening to the boys' conversation.

"Yeah, I happened to notice when I went up to the room to change just now."

"Did you tell Ms. Anderson and Mr. Robards about this?" Jen said, nearly tumbling off the sofa in her excitement.

Tommy looked embarrassed. "No, I didn't think it was important."

"Of course it's important!" Jen grabbed him by the arm and half dragged him to the reception desk.

"I still say it doesn't really mean anything," Tommy said defensively.

"It means *everything*," Jen insisted. "Don't you see? Jason's not playing a joke — he's heading for home!"

"You don't think he'd be crazy enough to hitchhike, do you?" Nora asked Ms. Anderson a few minutes later.

"I'm sure he wouldn't, but we have to cover every possibility," Ms. Anderson answered. "We've asked the police to check the major roads leading out of town. If they see him at the side of the road, they'll pick him up immediately."

She turned her attention back to her driving. The hotel manager had loaned her a hotel van, and she had taken Nora and five other girls with her to search for Jason. Mr. Robards, meanwhile, had called a cab, and along with two boys, was searching the neighborhood around the hotel.

"The awful part is," Ms. Anderson said quietly, "he could be anywhere. It's like trying to find a needle in a haystack. Where would a kid *go* if he was alone in Washington, D.C.?"

"Maybe an arcade?" Tracy said helpfully. "Jason loves video games."

"It's a possibility, I guess." She glanced at Tracy in the rearview mirror. "He won't have much money, though, and those places are expensive."

"Especially if he's been there all day," Nora said grimly.

"Poor Jason," Jen said sadly. "I wonder if he's even had anything to eat."

"That's it!" Tracy offered. "He's probably gone to an Italian restaurant. You know how much he loves pizza — all we have to do is figure out which restaurant he went to."

"Tracy," Nora said patiently, "do you know how many Italian restaurants there are in D.C.?"

"No, how many?"

Nora rolled her eyes to the ceiling of the van. "Too many for us to check, right, Ms. Anderson?"

"I'm afraid so." The light changed and the van shot forward. "But keep the ideas coming," she said encouragingly. "I need all the help I can get."

It wasn't until much later, when they were stopped at another red light, that they got the break that led them to Jason. Nora was staring wearily out the window when a bright yellow neon sign caught her eye.

"Look over on the left," she said excitedly, "it says, 'Bus Terminal.'"

For a moment, there was no response, and then Ms. Anderson's face lit up. "That's it — a bus terminal!" she cried. "The one place we haven't tried."

"And it makes sense," Jen said happily. "If he's really serious about going home, maybe that's where he went."

As soon as the light changed, Ms. Anderson made a three-point U-turn while the tires screeched. "Keep your fingers crossed, everybody," she pleaded. "This could be it." She pulled the van into a parking space and jumped out with the keys in her hand. "C'mon gang. As soon as we get inside, spread out and look for him."

The bus terminal was a dismal sight at ten o'clock, and they stood for a moment in the doorway, letting their eyes adjust to the harsh fluorescent light. And then Jen spotted Jason.

"That's him!" she yelled, pointing to a small figure at the far end of the terminal, slumped into a wooden seat. She and Tracy were the first to reach him, and they stood for a moment, looking at the still body clutching a worn suitcase.

"He's dead!" Tracy cried.

Jason's eyes flew open, and he sat bolt upright, blinking rapidly. "What time does the bus leave?" he asked thickly.

"He's not dead," Ms. Anderson laughed. She leaned over and ran her hand through Jason's tousled red hair. "He was just sleeping."

Chapter 13

"Jason, why did you do it?" Jen's eyes were warm with sympathy as she stared at him across the chipped vinyl table in Burger-To-Go. After the dramatic scene at the bus station, Ms. Anderson had stashed Jason's suitcase in the van, and taken everyone to the all-night diner across the street.

"It's hard to explain," Jason said vaguely. He finished the last of his double-fudge milk shake, and the straw made a loud slurping sound against the glass. Jason's ordeal hasn't hurt his appetite, Nora thought wryly. In the past fifteen minutes, he'd consumed two milk shakes and a double cheeseburger with onions.

"Another malted?" Ms. Anderson said, ready to signal the waitress.

"I couldn't," Jason said, leaning back against the seat contentedly. His eyes roamed over the pastries displayed in a glass refrigerator case. "I think I could eat a piece of that lemon meringue pie, though," he said thoughtfully.

"No problem," Ms. Anderson said, leaping to her feet. "I'll get it myself. And I just remembered I forgot to call Mr. Robards," she said.

"Won't he still be out somewhere in the taxi?" Tracy asked.

"Probably, but I can leave a message with the desk clerk," Ms. Anderson explained. She headed for a pay phone in the back of the diner, while Tracy looked at Jason in amazement.

"I can't *believe* you did this to everyone," Tracy said reproachfully. "You should see how upset Ms. Anderson and Mr. Robards were at dinner. They didn't even *eat* when they realized you were missing." She stared pointedly at the empty glasses and plates in front of Jason. "You still have *your* famous appetite, I see."

Jason's pale face suddenly reddened. "I know I caused a lot of trouble," he said shakily.

"Hah! That's the understatement of the year," Tracy snorted.

"Tracy!" Jen said protestingly. "He said he's sorry." She glanced at Jason who seemed to be on the verge of tears.

"But what *did* happen?" Tracy persisted. "Was this all just a joke, a game? Did you really expect us to find you here?"

"No, it wasn't like that," Jason said quickly.

"Then what *was* it like?" Amy Williams said curiously. "What would you have done if we hadn't showed up?"

"I guess I would have gone back to the hotel, because I didn't have enough money for a bus — " he broke off as Ms. Anderson slid back into her seat, and handed him a piece of pie.

"I left a message at the hotel," she said cheerfully. "I wish I could see Mr. Robards' face when he gets it," she added. "He's going to be so excited to find out that you're okay," she said warmly to Jason.

To her surprise, Jason's eyes filled with tears. "I'm — I'm really sorry about what happened," he said brokenly. "I didn't want to cause anybody any trouble — honestly. All I wanted was to go home."

"You wanted to go home?" Lucy asked. "That's what this is all about?"

Jason nodded, and wiped his hand across his eyes. "I guess it's hard for you guys to understand . . ." he said quietly. "But this has been the worst thing I've ever gone through."

"Tell us about it, Jason," Ms. Anderson urged gently.

He shrugged and stared at his empty plate. "I don't know if I can explain it, but . . . this is the first time I've ever been away from home."

"Really? You mean you've never gone to camp or anything like that?" Nora asked.

"Never. When I got the chance to go on this trip, I thought it would be really exciting. I figured it would be great staying at a hotel with the kids and eating out all the time." He paused and fiddled with a straw. "But then once I got here, I knew I had made a big mistake. All I could think about was getting back home." Ms. Anderson gave a little gasp of surprise, and Jason added quickly, "Not that you and Mr. Robards haven't been great — you really have. It's just that. . . ." He glanced at Jen helplessly.

"You were homesick," she said promptly.

Jason smiled sheepishly. "Sounds pretty silly, doesn't it?"

Everyone was quiet for a moment, and then Amy said firmly, "I don't think it's silly at all. When I was eight, I was so homesick at camp, I forged a note from my mother saying that I had to be sent home immediately." She giggled. "I even put a stamp on it, and drew little squiggly lines over it, like it had gone through the post office."

"What happened?" Tracy asked. "Did the people at the camp fall for it?"

"Not for a minute," Amy said ruefully. "In the first place, I had too many misspelled words, and let me give you a tip — if you're going to forge a note from your mother, don't write it on Snoopy paper."

"A good point," Ms. Anderson said, as everyone laughed.

"I remember when I was supposed to spend a whole month with my aunt on Cape Cod one summer," Jen said thoughtfully. "Everybody thought it would be great for me to be at the shore, but it didn't work out that way. I missed Dad and Eric and Jeff so much, I cried myself to sleep every night." She laughed. "Finally, my aunt got so sick of my moping around, she sent me home a week early." She looked around the table. "And now when we go to the shore, all four of us go!"

"I know how you feel, Jason," Nora said after a moment. "I can still remember the first time I spent the night away from home. Sally took me into New York with her for the weekend to see the Joffrey ballet."

"What was it like?" Lucy asked, spooning up her hot fudge sundae.

"I have no idea," Nora said with a smile. "Sally said I'm the only person she knows who cried all the way through *Swan Lake*!"

"Gosh," Tracy said slowly, "it was *that* sad?"

There was a burst of laughter around the table, and then Jen said consolingly, "I'll explain it to you later, Tracy."

"Well, Jason, it looks like you're not the first person in the world to get homesick," Ms. Anderson said. Her green eyes swept around the table. "In fact, it sounds like everybody here has experienced it."

"What about you, Ms. Anderson?" Amy Williams asked.

"Don't be silly," Tracy said, reaching for a cherry Coke. "Grown-ups don't get homesick."

"Oh, yes they do!" Ms. Anderson said firmly. "In fact, I remember my first day at Cedar Groves. I was so miserable, I wanted to hide in the ladies' room and cry my eyes out."

"But how could *you* be homesick?" Jason said wonderingly. "You're a teacher."

"Believe me, it happens, Jason," Ms. Anderson said ruefully. She squinted and pushed her glasses back on her nose. "I had just moved to town that week, and Cedar

Groves was my very first teaching assignment. I didn't know *anybody*, and I missed all my friends from college."

"It must have been really hard for you," Jen told her.

"It was," Ms. Anderson admitted. "It seemed like one day I was a student, and the next day — bingo! I was a teacher. Just like that!" She sipped her iced tea thoughtfully. "And as you all know," she said kiddingly, "teachers are supposed to know *everything* and never make mistakes. So I was afraid to open my mouth or ask questions." She sighed. "I just wandered around the halls on my own."

"Did you ever get lost?" Nora piped up.

"Constantly! And I misplaced my class schedule the very first day I got it. So I stumbled around all week wondering where I was supposed to go next."

"You could have gotten another schedule from the office," Mia pointed out.

"Hah!" Ms. Anderson rolled her eyes. "Can you imagine what our very efficient school secretary would have said?"

Jen and Nora exchanged an amused look. Who would ever think that even a *teacher* would be afraid of going to the school office?

Later, in the van, Jason said quietly, "You guys must think I'm the biggest jerk in the world."

"No, we don't," Nora assured him. "We've all been in your shoes before," she said, looking at her friends.

"That's right," Jen agreed. "Everybody has a first time away from home. In fact, if you took a poll, I bet most kids would admit that they've been homesick at some time in their lives."

"They just never did anything as drastic as you did, Jason," Tracy offered.

A slow smile spread over Jason's freckled face. "I always like to do things with style," he kidded.

Ms. Anderson heard the last comment and made a wry face. "Just promise me there won't be a repeat performance, Jason," she said, pulling up in front of the hotel. "I feel like I've aged ten years tonight!"

"I promise you I'll never do anything like this again," Jason said solemnly. Then he winked at Nora, who was sitting next to him. "At least, not on this trip," he added softly.

"Congratulations," a male voice said, as Nora headed for the elevator a few minutes later. "Your second rescue of the day!"

Nora turned to see Brad Hartley staring at her with an appraising look in his brown eyes.

"I can't take the credit for finding Jason," she said stiffly. "It was just lucky that we happened to pass the bus terminal." As usual, Brad was making fun of her, she decided, but tonight, she felt too weary to retaliate.

"Hey, I'm serious," Brad said quickly, sensing her mood. He took a step closer and touched her gently on the arm. "I wasn't being sarcastic. You know, I thought it was really super what you did on the parkway today." He laughed as they crossed the lobby together. "If it weren't for you, we might still be sitting there in a smoking van."

"I doubt that," Nora said, giving him a shy smile.

"You never know," he said seriously. "And tonight . . . I heard that it was your idea to check the bus station for Jason."

"Well, it was a pretty obvious choice," Nora said, embarrassed by his praise. "Ms. Anderson just happened to drive by it, and. . . ."

"You're too modest," he said, grinning at her. He pressed the elevator button and moved closer to her. "Do you think I could call you when we get back to Cedar Groves?"

"Call me?" Nora stammered. She

couldn't believe her ears. Was he asking her out?

"Yes, call you," he repeated. "Like, on the telephone," he said, holding an imaginary phone up to his ear, just as a bunch of kids appeared beside them.

"I — yes, of course," Nora blurted out, the words tumbling over each other. They were separated when the elevator doors opened, and the crowd surged forward. "Yes!" she said loudly, her eyes meeting his over the sea of faces.

"Good," he mouthed. He turned away just then, when Mitch Pauley said something to him, but not before he gave her a long, special look.

Wait till I tell Jen about this! Nora thought excitedly. *Brad Hartley wants to* call *me!*

"Jen, are you awake?" Nora whispered cautiously later that night. It was a little after eleven, and Tracy and Lucy were sound asleep in the darkened hotel room.

"I am now," a muffled voice responded from under the covers.

"Well, that's good, because I've got something important to tell you," Nora said. She paused dramatically. "It's about Brad Hartley." There was no answer from the figure under the blanket, and she gave it an impatient nudge. "It's about Brad Hartley . . . and me."

"Ouch! I heard you the first time," Jen complained, and turned over on her stomach. "What's the big news?"

Nora gave a quick look at the adjoining bed where the other two girls were sleeping. She wasn't ready to share her news about Brad with them — not yet.

Nora took a deep breath. "I think he asked me out."

"What!" Jen flipped over on her back, and her eyes flew wide open like a zombie's. "He asked you out!"

"Shhh," Nora said warningly. "I don't want the whole world to know about it."

"Well, tell me what happened," Jen said, propping herself up on an elbow. "What do you mean, you *think* he asked you out?"

"It's hard to know for sure," Nora said hesitantly. She quickly explained the situation to Jen and then said cautiously, "Do you think he meant something else?"

Jen's bubbly laughter escaped from the covers. "What else would he mean, silly? Do you think he wants to call you up just to say hi, or to get help with his shop homework?" She sat straight up in bed then, and looked at her friend very seriously. "Believe me, Brad's going to ask you out."

"Do you really think so?" Nora whispered back.

"I know so." Jen paused. "The question is, What are you going to do about it?"

It was exciting . . . and terrifying. Her first real date. What would she do, what would she say? She could feel her stomach churning, just thinking about it.

"What are you going to do?" Jen repeated.

"I don't know!" Nora blurted out. "If he asks me out, I'll . . . I'll just die!"

"Don't be silly," Jen said calmly. "When he asks you out, you'll say yes." She flipped back on her stomach and drew the blanket over her shoulders. "Now go back to sleep," she muttered thickly. "We'll talk about it tomorrow."

The next morning, Nora remembered the stolen dinner roll, safely tucked away in her night table, and decided to surprise her friends.

"Okay, you guys, brace yourself for a shock," she said, reaching into the drawer. "I've got a confession to make. I've been holding out on you."

"What do you mean?" Tracy said.

"I mean I've got a fantastic surprise for you," Nora said, beaming. "We've got a little souvenir from Trilogy."

"Ooh, what is it?" Tracy cried.

"It's . . . it's gone!" Nora's smile faded as her hand hit the bottom of the empty drawer.

"What's gone?" Lucy asked, interested.

"The dinner roll," Nora said, dropping to her hands and knees and frantically searching under the night table. "But that's impossible. It couldn't have disappeared — it just couldn't!"

"What's so important about a roll?" Tracy asked nervously.

"The roll was the souvenir," Nora said, between gritted teeth. "I took it off Trilogy's dinner tray that night we went up to the penthouse. I wanted to surprise you with it, and now it's gone!"

"Don't get upset, Nora," Lucy said gently. "After all, if it was left on the dinner tray, it probably means that Trilogy didn't even touch it."

"No, someone had taken a little bite out of it," Tracy said helpfully, and then clapped her hand over her mouth.

"What did you say?" Nora wheeled around furiously. "Tracy, do you know something about this?"

"I . . . was in the room alone for a while last night, and I was looking for a bobby pin," Tracy explained.

"Go on." Nora folded her arms across

her chest, and braced herself to expect the worst.

"And . . . I looked in the drawer, and there it was." Tracy stopped and her lower lip was trembling. "The roll, I mean."

"And I suppose it flew away?" Nora said sarcastically.

"No," Tracy said miserably. "I . . . ate it."

"You ate it!" Nora gasped.

"Yes, I ate it," Tracy said. "I was starving! I had no idea you were saving it." She looked up at Jen and Lucy. "You've got to believe me. If I had known that it belonged to Trilogy, I wouldn't have touched it. Anyway," she added, "if it makes you feel any better, I didn't even *enjoy* it. It was hard as a rock!"

"I can't believe this," Nora muttered, her hands dropping limply at her sides. She remembered the heart-stopping fear, the crazy excitement as they sneaked up to the penthouse . . . and now it was all for nothing! Their only souvenir of the experience was gone forever.

For a long moment, no one said anything, and then Lucy, with a twinkle in her dark eyes, gave a long sigh. "Oh well," she said mischievously, "easy come, easy go."

Chapter 14

Nora had been back in Cedar Groves for two days when "the call" from Brad finally came. She had rehearsed what she'd say to him, but when she heard his deep voice on the phone, all her lines flew out of her head. Luckily, Brad didn't expect any brilliant dialogue from her — the call was brief and to the point. Would she like to go for pizza and a movie on Saturday night? Giddy with excitement, Nora accepted.

"You think I did the right thing, don't you?" she asked Jen worriedly. It was Friday afternoon, and they were going through Nora's closet, trying to find just the right outfit for her to wear on her date.

"Of course I do," Jen said, sifting through a pile of sweaters that Nora had stashed on her closet shelf. "Nora," she said, giggling, "you have got to be the most organized person I know. I can't believe you actually arrange your sweaters by *color*."

Nora shook her head. "I don't understand it," she moaned. "I've got a ton of clothes and nothing to wear!"

"Hmmm," Jen said thoughtfully. "Nothing seems quite right for tomorrow night, does it?"

"No," Nora answered, dismayed. "I never thought going on a date could be this complicated." She sat down on her closet floor and surveyed her shoes. "And clothes are the least of my worries!"

"What do you mean?" Jen said, dropping down beside her.

"Well, there are a lot of other things to think about. Like, what are Brad and I going to *talk* about?"

Jen thought for a moment. "The same stuff you and I talk about, I guess."

"Like what to wear on dates?" Nora countered.

"Oh, you know what I mean," Jen retorted. "You can talk about lots of things."

"Name one."

"Well, um, things that are happening at school."

"Like shop class?" Nora raised a skeptical eyebrow. "Do you want me to give him a few pointers on mechanics?"

"No, of course not," Jen said hastily.

"You know, you can always talk about books and movies."

"I don't know what he likes."

"Then this is your chance to find out," Jen said cheerfully. "The same as it is for him. Honestly, Nora, I think you're worrying too much. Thousands of people go on dates every single day. What do they find to talk about?"

"I don't know," Nora said morosely. "I've often wondered."

"How did he sound on the phone?" Jen asked. "Did he have a lot to say?"

"Not really. I was so excited, it was kind of a blur, but I know it didn't take long. He just asked me if I wanted to go out, and then when I said yes, he told me he'd pick me up at seven. I'm really getting worried. What if we just sit there all night and have nothing to say to each other?"

Jen pondered this for a moment, and then brightened. "You're going to Luigi's for dinner, right?"

"Right."

"So order a large Sicilian pizza with peppers and extra cheese. It'll take ages to eat, and you won't have time to talk much."

"Very funny." Nora paused and then said seriously, "What if he . . . at the end of the evening . . . you know. . . ."

"No, I don't know," Jen said innocently.

"When he says good-night," Nora said impatiently, "what if he tries to. . . ."

"Kiss you?"

Nora nodded. "What should I do?"

"I don't know. What do you want to do?"

Nora thought for a moment. "If I really, *really* liked him, maybe it would be okay." She drew her knees up to her chest and wrapped her arms around her legs. "But the idea kind of scares me. Would it scare you?"

"You want the truth?" Jen asked. "Yeah, it would scare me." She gave Nora a friendly punch on the arm. "But aren't you rushing things a little? Maybe he has no intention of kissing you. In fact, you know what would be funny? Maybe Brad's worrying, right this minute, about what *he's* going to say to you!"

"Somehow I doubt that," Nora muttered. "I don't think boys worry about things like that."

Jen sighed and stood up. "Well, you never know, Nora," she said, sifting through a pile of sweaters. "You just never know."

On Saturday evening, Nora's room looked like someone was holding a rummage sale in it. She had changed her clothes five times before finally deciding to go with her first choice, a tailored khaki skirt and a long-sleeved red blouse.

"Yes, definitely. Go with that," Jen said, scrutinizing her in the mirror. She suddenly burrowed under a pile of blouses on Nora's bed, and held up a length of tan macrame. "But wear this belt with it. It saves it from being boring."

"Boring?" Nora muttered. "At the moment, I'd be happy to be boring. I think I'm going to die of nervousness before he even gets here."

"I told you to eat some lunch," Jen said reproachfully. "How could you turn down Jeff's macaroni casserole? It was super."

"Please," Nora said weakly, "I don't even want to think about food. My stomach's doing somersaults."

"Then you're going to have a real problem at Luigi's tonight," Jen told her.

"I know," Nora said, paling. "I'll have to order the smallest thing on the menu."

Jen hooted. "The smallest thing on the menu is a giant Italian sub!" She glanced at the clock on Nora's night table and grabbed her jacket. "Hey, I've got to go. Brad's going to be here any second. Good luck!" she added, bolting for the door.

"Jen!" Nora wailed.

"Yes?" Jen asked, with one hand on the doorknob.

"I'm scared," Nora said, her mouth dry. "You don't suppose there's any way I could get out of it?"

"Nope," Jen said cheerfully, just as the doorbell rang.

Nora froze in her tracks. "That's him!"

Jen gave Nora's arm a final squeeze. "Have fun," she whispered and disappeared into the hall.

"Fun?" Nora mouthed, staring at her reflection in the mirror. "I'm going to have a heart attack!"

"Are you sure you like Italian food?" Brad asked half an hour later. There had been a moment's confusion over who would sit where when they slid into the back booth at Luigi's. Finally, they sat across from each other, and Nora nervously folded and unfolded her napkin on her lap.

"I love it!" she said brightly. "In fact, I've been looking forward to this all day." As soon as the words were out, she wanted to bite her tongue off. What a dumb thing to say! He'd think she meant she was looking forward to seeing *him* all day. "Eating Italian food, I mean," she mumbled. Great, now she sounded rude. She could feel herself flushing, and suddenly Brad was on his feet.

"I should have hung up your coat," he apologized.

"Oh, that's all right, I'll just keep it," she said, clutching the coat around her shoulders like she was warding off an Arctic wind.

"But Nora, it's hot in here," Brad protested. "Look at you; your face is all red."

"All right," Nora muttered grimly. Silently, Nora tried to wriggle out of the light raincoat she'd borrowed from Sally. Her watch got caught in the sleeve, and for one awful moment, her hands were trapped behind her back while Brad tried unsuccessfully to free her.

When the coat was finally hung up, Brad sat down and the two of them studied the menu.

"Everything looks good," Nora said, wishing she could summon up an appetite.

"It sure does," Brad agreed. "Do you want to split a pizza?"

"Fine with me," Nora answered, forcing some enthusiasm into her voice. She remembered what Jen had said about ordering a large pizza and smiled. It was going to take more than a pizza to save this conversation!

Later, at the movie, Nora relaxed a little. Not having to talk all the time took the pressure off, and by the middle of the film, she and Brad were laughing as they passed the popcorn back and forth.

"I had no idea you liked horror movies," Brad whispered happily.

"Like them? I sat through *Bride of Dracula* eight times!"

"*Bride of Dracula*?" Brad said, nodding his head approvingly. He sipped his drink thoughtfully. "How about the early *Godzilla* movies?"

"Fantastic," Nora said warmly. "Remember Megatron?"

"Who could forget him?"

When the movie was over, and they were walking home, it seemed like the most natural thing in the world for Brad to hold her hand. A light rain had started to fall, and they hopscotched their way down the sidewalk.

"It's kind of nice to see you away from school," Brad said thoughtfully. "Not that it's not nice to see you *in* school," he added quickly. He pulled her a little closer to him, as they waited for a traffic light to change, and Nora discovered that she didn't mind it one bit. "You seem more serious in school," he said. "But tonight, you seem different."

"In what way?" she asked.

"More fun." The light changed, and he

grabbed her hand tightly as they crossed the street. "A little crazy and unpredictable. Definitely more fun."

"You want fun?" Nora challenged him. "I'll show you fun!" Before he could answer, she jumped off the curb and landed in a giant puddle. Brad jumped back, but not quite fast enough, and the spray from the puddle caught him on the ankles.

"Hey!" he protested. "I wanted fun, not a tidal wave!"

Nora grinned. "I'm just crazy and unpredictable," she teased him.

"You splashed each other?" Jen said later in a puzzled voice. "That's his idea of fun?" She sighed and cradled the Princess phone against her ear. She'd been talking to Nora for the past fifteen minutes, but Nora was giggling so much, it was hard to find out what really happened on her date.

"You'd have to be there to understand," Nora said, gasping with laughter. "I really can't explain it."

"I take it you had a good time," Jen said dryly.

"It was fantastic," Nora answered in a bubbly voice. "The best time of my whole life!"

"Isn't that a little extreme?"

"Nope." There was a loud crunch while Nora bit into an apple. "It was like a dream."

A dream. Jen had been sprawled in front of the television for hours, watching one dumb sitcom after another, wondering if the evening would ever end. She'd felt alone, left out . . . and maybe a little jealous, she thought guiltily. She forced a laugh.

Nora said happily, "Brad was great, the date was great, everything was great!"

Jen sighed. The idea of a date still seemed scary and grown-up to her, but Nora sounded like she'd just come off a roller coaster ride. It's funny, she mused, we've always shared everything before, but there's something different about tonight. What was it Nora had said? You had to be there to understand? Well, that was just it. She hadn't been there — she'd been stuck at home watching a *Gilligan's Island* rerun while Nora was out having the time of her life! There was a pause, and then Jen said softly, "What about the big moment? Any problems?"

"The big — oh, you mean when he kissed me good-night," Nora said blithely. "No, no problems on that score." She gave a little giggle, imagining what her friend's reaction would be.

"What!" Jen yelled. "He kissed you good-night, and you didn't even tell me! Nora Ryan, you've been holding out on me. I'm not going to forget this!"

"I wasn't holding out, Jen, honest. It just slipped my mind." She took another bite out of her apple. She wondered why she was so hungry and then remembered that she'd been too nervous to eat at dinner.

"I bet." Jen waited a moment and then asked, "So what was it like?"

"The kiss? We were worrying for nothing," Nora said calmly. "It went okay. We didn't bump noses or anything. And it was over with before I knew it."

"Did he ask you if he could?"

"No, he just leaned over and kissed me when we got to the front door." Nora leaned back in bed and hugged her pillow to her chest. This had been the most exciting night of her life, and it was great to have a best friend to share it with. Except she was sure that something was bothering Jen. Nothing she could pinpoint exactly. Maybe a hint of uncertainty in her voice and those long, thoughtful pauses in the conversation. Was she imagining it? She brushed the idea aside and spent the next few minutes talking about the movie.

"Well, I'm glad everything went okay," Jen said finally. "I thought about you all night. I had my fingers crossed."

This time there was no mistaking the sadness in her voice, and Nora understood. Jen feels left out! she realized with a jolt. She wondered what she could say to reassure her. "Well, believe me, I had mine crossed, too. I was really a nervous wreck when I left the house — "

"I know, I was there," Jen reminded her.

"But somehow everything worked out okay." She paused. "It'll be that way for you, too, you know."

"What do you mean?"

Nora laughed. "Well, you'll probably be next, you know."

"What!"

"You'll probably be the next one to go on a date," Nora said calmly.

"You've got to be kidding," Jen said feelingly. "I don't even know anybody who'd ask me out."

"That's what *I* thought," Nora told her. "But boys have a way of surprising you. And was Tracy ever wrong! I would have felt *really* dumb tonight, if Brad had asked me out because he *thought* I was dumb!"

"Yeah," said Jen. "How dumb can you get? But if somebody asks me out, I'll die," she went on solemnly.

"No you won't," Nora laughed. "The thing to remember is not to take it too seriously. . . ." She burrowed into the pillow and brought the comforter up to her chin. "And just remember, the boy's probably as nervous as you are."

"Brad didn't seem to be nervous," Jen pointed out.

Nora considered this for a moment. "Maybe he was, but he's just better at covering it up. Or maybe he was a basket case *before* he left the house. . . ." She laughed. "Or maybe he had a great friend like you — someone who helped him figure out what to wear and what to say."

"Hah! I doubt it. Anyway, I wasn't that much help."

"Are you nuts?" Nora said, sitting up suddenly and flinging off the covers. "I couldn't have made it without you, Jen, and that's the truth! I would have called the whole thing off."

"No you wouldn't have. You would have managed. You always do."

"Not this time," Nora said feelingly. "I would have had an anxiety attack, right in the middle of Luigi's. I might have fainted, facedown in the middle of the mushroom-and-pepper pizza."

Jen giggled. "If you say so. . . ."

"I say so," Nora said firmly. "You saved my life tonight. And someday soon, I'll be returning the favor for you."

"We'll have to wait and see about that," Jen said, shyly pleased. She felt good about everything again. She had been part of Nora's evening after all. Secretly, she wondered if she really would be next. What would it be like, going on a date? Would it be scary, would it be wonderful?

She knew that whatever happened, Nora would be right there to help her. To go through her closet with her, give her hints on what to talk about. . . . And most importantly, to rehash the evening later.

She sighed and reached for a bag of potato chips. Now that everything was okay, she could relax. "So tell me about the movie again," she said to Nora. "What happened to the stalled subway cars when the monster ate Tokyo?"

"Oh, you mean the part where Brad held my hand?" Nora asked. "That was the most exciting part of all, but it's kind of a long story. Do you have time to hear it?"

Jen snuggled under her quilt, warm and toasty in her nightshirt. "All the time in the world," she said happily.

If Jen had wanted help, wouldn't she have asked for it? Read Junior High #5, THE EIGHTH GRADE TO THE RESCUE.